RIVALS ON THE RANCH
GUNPOWDER

RIVALS ON THE RANCH
GUNPOWDER

WRITTEN BY MICHAEL ROUNTREE WITH LORI WILDE
ILLUSTRATED BY PEYTON AUFILL

Interior Design and Formatting by:

www.emtippettsbookdesigns.com

*In memory of my grandparents Homer Lee
and Alice Elizabeth Brumley.*

TABLE OF CONTENTS

BIG SHARP HORNS

Howdy, partner, it's Gunpowder, your favorite cowpony. At least I hope I'm your favorite. Pull up a feed bucket, flip it over, and have a seat, because I've got a story to tell!

It was a nice fall Texas day and the air was cool. The kind of day that makes a horse want to take off running full blast, kicking and bucking, just because it feels so good to be alive.

The mesquite trees were dropping their leaves and baring big old thorns that could rip and poke the hides of kids and cowponies alike. My hair grew thicker as I put on my winter coat for the coming cold weather. Cowboys and cowgirls hung up their straw hats and got out their felts, their way of putting on for the winter, too.

Coming home from Cowboy School, Conrad and I ambled down the country road, and through the gate of Mesquite Bean Ranch.

As we neared the house, the two ranch dogs, Maggie and Tuffy, jumped up from their afternoon nap, yapping like the barn was on fire.

"Bark, bark, bark."

The hairs on their backs bristled up as if we were invaders come to steal something valuable, like a bale of hay or bag of oats.

I'm not sure who they were trying to impress. We were the only ones around besides a fat horned toad eating dinner in the middle of a big red ant bed.

Conrad stopped me and raised his hands in surrender. "We give up, don't bite!"

Cautiously, the dogs approached. They stuck their noses up and sniffed the air until they caught our familiar scent. Their bristled hair went down and their ears drooped and their fangs disappeared.

Conrad shook his head and grinned. "You crazy dogs! Y'all do this every day. When will you learn it's us?"

Tails wagging, the dogs followed us to the barn. Conrad unsaddled me and left me munching on an after-school snack of fine alfalfa hay. He ran into the house for his own snack.

Tuffy and Maggie sat down in the barn doorway, tongues lolling, soaking up the sun. In the stall next to me stood a big roan gelding that belonged to the ranch foreman, Mr. Winks.

Old Roany was one of the toughest, wisest cowponies in this part of Texas.

"How was Cowboy School?" he asked.

"Normal day of books, roping, and riding," I said. "Why the sudden interest in my day? You don't usually ask."

2

I can't let my guard down with Roany because he was often out to "teach me a lesson" if you know what I mean.

"How can a horse learn from books?" He snorted.

"That's not what I mean, and you know it. Conrad learns from books. Then we ride and rope and do horse things. That's the way Cowboy School works."

Roany slid me a sly, sideways glance that let me know he was just trying to get a rise out of me.

"Where's Mr. Winks? I thought we were working the fall calves this afternoon," I asked.

"Smart as you are, I thought for sure you'd know exactly where he is." Roany's eyes narrowed, sizing me up.

I switched my ears back and forth, and raised one eyebrow. "Just tell me."

"He had to go to Brownwood to buy some horseshoes,

nails, and fencing supplies, so sit tight."

Dang. Mr. Winks had gone to town? I really had my heart set on working calves that afternoon.

Bam!

The screen door slammed and here came Conrad like a Texas tornado, shuffling along, dragging his boots, clanking his spurs, chewing on a piece of jerky. His felt hat tilted back on his head.

I nickered softly.

"Mr. Winks is off somewhere. Let's go on out to the pasture and start working calves." Conrad said. "I'll leave him a note on the tack room door telling him where we went."

I bobbed my head, letting him know I was on board.

Conrad got the tack, slipped a bridle over my ears, and looped the reins over the hitching post. He put his lasso, medicine bag, and piggin' string over the saddle horn.

In case you don't remember from my other tales, a piggin' string is a small rope that is used to tie a calf's legs, so he can't run away when a cowhand needs to doctor him.

Conrad put his left boot in the stirrup, pulled up, and swung his leg over my back. Away we went.

Roany neighed and pawed the ground at us to stop and come back. He didn't want us going off without Mr. Winks.

I neighed back telling him things would be just fine and that he worried too much. I popped my tail and might even have stuck my tongue out at him.

We took off across the pasture in search of new baby calves. Mr. Winks liked to rope and vaccinate them as soon as they are born. It was exciting to watch brand-new babies stagger up off the ground, wobble around on their new legs, and bellow for their mamas.

Most of the time their mamas would bellow back and just watch us. They're used to cowhands and cowponies, and they know we wouldn't hurt their calves.

Occasionally, we would get an overly protective mama, and she'll flat put up a fight. But we knew who those cows were. If we came across them, we would wait for Mr. Winks and Roany to help us.

Sometimes, a cow would hide her newborn calf close to some brush or a tree. But, by the time they are two or three days old, they are up and around and following their mamas.

We sifted through the mesquite trees.

Up ahead, we spotted a calf right out in the open. Conrad

built a loop with his rope. "Let's go, Gunpowder."

Spurs jingling, Conrad stood up in the saddle and readied his rope to swing.

The mama and her calf stood looking at us as we rode up. They didn't even try to run away. This was going to be easy.

"Brrrr," bellowed the mama cow. "Brrr, brrr."

I wasn't sure if it was a welcome bellow or a warning. But the sound rolled off her lips soft and low, so I wasn't too worried.

Conrad swung his rope a couple of times and gently tossed the loop around the calf's neck.

At this point, my job was to stay alert and watch for anything that might interfere with Conrad doing his job. That "anything" was usually the mama cow.

I kept my ears pitched forward and my eyes wide open, focused on that mama.

"Come over here, little doggie," Conrad coaxed.

He grabbed the medicine bag from where it hung around the saddle horn and dismounted. Baby calves can get very sick in their first few weeks of life, and vaccines help keep them well. Easily, he flanked the weak newborn calf and gave it two injections. A tetanus shot and one for the flu.

"Brrrrrr!" the mama warned.

I backed both ears, barred my teeth at her, making it very clear she would have to go through me to get to Conrad.

That cow got real smart, real quickly. She took three steps backward.

Conrad heard the commotion, but just glanced over his shoulder and grinned. He had complete confidence in me, and knew I would keep him safe. We had been working as a team for a long time.

In two shakes of a rabbit's tail, Conrad finished giving the vaccines, untied the calf, and let it up.

That calf shook to get the grass off. He bellowed for his mama and ran to her.

I don't speak baby calf too well, but I'm sure that bellow said: *What the heck just happened? These strange looking creatures came up and woke me from my nap. They roped me, tied three of my legs together, stuck me in the skin with a couple of sharp things, and then let me go.*

Does sound kind of strange, doesn't it?

Conrad climbed back into the saddle. Since the fall days were getting shorter and we only had about an hour of daylight left, there wasn't much time left to catch more calves.

And there was still no sign of Mr. Winks and Roany.

"Gunpowder," Conrad said. "Why don't we circle around to the west fence and head back to the ranch house? That way if we run across any new calves, we'll vaccinate them along the way and call it a day."

We trotted off to the west, but didn't see a single cow or calf. I figured we were all done for the day, when a few feet over to the left, I saw the bushes shake.

"Whoa, Gunpowder." Conrad pulled back on the reins. "Looks like we have one more."

"Brrrr."

We heard the calf but could only make out a small shadow of the baby lying on the ground. The mama had to be close, but there was no sign of her.

I got a weird feeling in my withers and the hairs on my back bristled. Things had gone too well this afternoon. Something wasn't right.

"Whoa, Gunpowder, be still," Conrad said. "I have to get my medicine bag and work this calf."

Not knowing where the baby's mama was hiding set my nerves on edge like a long-tailed cat in a room full of rocking chairs.

"It's okay, Gunpowder, forget about that cow, and let's get this done, so we can get back home for dinner."

Thud. Thud. Thud. The ground shook.

My heart flew into my throat. I spun around.

There stood the largest-horned, meanest-looking, nastiest-acting tiger-striped cow. Her eyes were narrow, and her horns looked sharp.

Who was she? She definitely didn't fit into the Mesquite Bean herd. They were white-faced red Hereford and black Angus cattle. There was not a single tiger-stripe in our herd.

Usually in times of danger, I'm calm as a cucumber. It took a lot to rattle me.

But this cow had a lot of white in her eyes.

Roany once told me to watch out for cows and horses that have a lot of white in their eye. Too much white in the eyes means they could be a loco. Those loco cows don't have much compromise in their vocabulary. It's their way or no way.

She pawed the ground with her hoof and tossed those horns.

Uh-oh. Time to shake this cow up and show her who was boss of the pasture. She was going to have to learn like all the others that I was in charge here.

She lowered her head, let out a loud moo, and charged straight for Conrad.

Conrad's eyes were big as silver dollars, and he froze in his tracks with her calf in his arms.

Some brush and a small tree lay between the tiger-striped cow and Conrad, but she went right through it and bent that sapling right over.

"Snap out of it, Conrad, wake up!" I whinnied.

But he didn't move.

I turned my backside to him and gave him a good stinging swish in his face to break the spell, but it didn't faze him.

He just stood, open-mouthed and staring.

Mama cow was about five yards away. Nostrils flaring, eyes all white.

I gave her the warning signs first. You know, backing my ears, showing my teeth, wheeling around, showing that I wouldn't hesitate to kick her.

She didn't care. She came at us in a dead run, bellowing at the top of her lungs. She lowered her head and pointed her big scary horns at the enemy holding her baby.

Conrad.

Gulp! This was gonna hurt, but I had no choice. I had to protect him.

I lowered my head and nailed that cow in her side with both my hind hooves, using as much force as I could muster up.

Crash!

She landed in the middle of the biggest

patch of prickly pear cactus in the pasture.

That mama cow came up madder than mad and meaner than mean!

She stood there with about a hundred little cactus spines in her side, and she didn't even notice. All that mattered to her was her baby. She pawed the ground and shook her horns.

That scared me. I had no idea what she would do.

Conrad let go of her calf and high-tailed it to the tallest tree he could find. But as fast as he was, she was faster.

She surged after him, her left horn close enough to pick him up by the seat of his britches and toss him into the next county.

No way!

I charged. Collided with her at a dead run.

Smack!

I rolled off her hip and smashed against the fork of a

mesquite tree stump. A sharp sudden pain shot down my back. I lay on the ground, the air knocked out of me.

"Gunpowder!" yelled Conrad. "Get up! Get Up! She's coming back!"

I staggered to my feet.

She raked her sharp horn across my shoulder.

A screaming pain brought me to my knees. My temples pounded. I saw stars. Blood streamed from my shoulder. My legs wobbled, and I couldn't catch my breath.

But I only had one thought in my head.

Conrad.

Where was he?

I looked up to see Conrad screaming at that mean old cow from the top branch of an oak tree. He was safe. That was all that mattered.

He was safe and I was... I was...

My head spun, my knees buckled, and then it was lights out.

A Trip to the Vet Clinic

A small gentle hand rubbed my nose, and Conrad's calm voice said, "Wake up, wake up, Gunpowder."

Slowly, I blinked open my eyes.

It was completely dark except for the headlights of the ranch pickup shining on me. Mr. Winks and Conrad's dad, Herman, kneeled beside me.

My shoulder burned like liquid fire, and it was all I could do not to groan.

"Guys, this looks bad," Mr. Winks worried.

If it looked as bad as it felt, I was in big trouble.

"We've got to stop the bleeding." Mr. Winks looked grim. "And get Gunpowder to Doc Riley immediately."

The only memory I have of Doc Riley wasn't good. A couple of years back, I'd eaten green lawn clippings and got the colic. Doc Riley jammed a rubber tube up my nose, pushed it down to my stomach and pumped a bunch of solution into me.

Yes, it was just as miserable as it sounds. Doc Riley cured me all right, but he wasn't my favorite person. Now I had this image of ol' Doc Riley with a huge needle and thread that looked like bailing wire, ready to sew me up.

I gulped. While I'd survived the vicious attack by that mean cow, I wasn't sure if I'd survive the vet.

"Conrad," Mr. Winks went on. "You and I will hold Gunpowder's head down. Herman, you grab that burlap feed sack from behind the seat of my pickup."

Herman took off and came back real quick with that feed sack.

"Press the sack firmly against his wound and hold it while we load him into the trailer," Mr. Winks instructed.

I squirmed.

Conrad held my head in his lap and whispered in my ear, "Hang on, Gunpowder, we'll take care of you. This is gonna hurt, so be brave."

Herman pressed the burlap sack down on my wound. Hard.

Ow! My shoulder was hot and sticky with blood.

"Come on, Gunpowder," Herman coaxed, bearing down with both hands. "Get up, so we can load you."

My shoulder hurt so badly that I wanted to cry, but I managed to stagger to my feet. The step up into the trailer was like another horn in my side, and I balked. How much pain could one horse take in one day?

"Come on, old buddy," whispered Conrad. "You can do this."

Was he talking to me? I couldn't tell, my head was so fuzzy.

"Get in there," Mr. Winks commanded, sounding plenty worried. "You're losing too much blood, and we don't have time to waste. You could die if we don't get you to the vet in a hurry."

I knew he was right, but the pain was relentless. It hurt so badly that I got sick to my stomach.

"Herman," Mr. Winks said. "Grab the loop of my lasso and put it around Gunpowder's hips. We are gonna help him into the trailer," Mr. Winks climbed onto Roany's back.

Herman gently settled the loop around my rear and handed the other end of the rope to Mr. Winks.

The ranch foreman dallied the lasso around his saddle horn and guided Roany to the side of the trailer ahead of me. "Get ready everyone. We're gonna pull Gunpowder into the trailer."

I did not like the sound of that one bit. I set my haunches down and put every pound of horseflesh I could muster against the pull, but I was no match for the big, stout, muscular Roany.

My front legs trembled, and it was either take a step, or fall down. And falling down had to hurt worse than going forward. I had no choice. I bit my lip, mumbled a few choice words about Roany, and up I went with a loud squeal.

That ten-mile journey to the vet clinic felt like a hundred. Herman stood beside me all the way, holding his hands against the wound to stop the bleeding. My head throbbed, and my shoulder felt every bump in the road. I pressed my lips together to keep from moaning.

Fifteen minutes later, Mr. Winks pulled up to the vet's office. Conrad and Mr. Winks guided me out of the trailer. I slowly backed out, feeling the jarring pain with every step. I put both back legs on the ground, then the left front and then the right.

A white haired man with gray whiskers came out to greet us. "Howdy, Gunpowder, remember me? I'm Doc Riley."

Did he really think I could forget? The previous visit to his clinic was etched into my memory.

But something was different about him. He had the same worn, stained cowboy hat pushed back on his head. His sleeves were rolled up like usual, and he wore his battered cowboy boots and faded jeans. But this time, unlike when I'd met him before, he smiled kindly.

That smile worried me more than a frown. Was I so bad off that even grumpy ole' Doc Riley was being nice to me?

"Let me take a look at that nasty cut. I hear you were pretty brave out in the pasture." He bent down.

I squirmed and sidestepped.

"It's okay, bud. I'll be as gentle as I can."

Conrad doffed his hat and worried the brim with his fingers. "Is he gonna be okay?"

Doc Riley put his hand on Conrad's shoulder. "Son, I believe we can patch him up, and after a long rest, he should be as good as new. Bring him in the clinic barn, and I'll get to work on him."

Get to work on me! Hmph. Did he think I was a pickup truck that needed an oil change?

The clinic was a big open barn that had stalls on one side for horses, and pens on the other for cattle, sheep, and goats. In the middle there was a concrete slab with rubber mats and a water faucet close by.

Doc Riley washed out the wound with cold water. I jumped and shivered, but it felt good to get that sticky blood off.

Then came the needles. They weren't a foot long like I had imagined. They were regular size. Still, it didn't make me feel any better. A shot was a shot.

"Hold still, Gunpowder, and I'll be gentle." Doc Riley stuck the needle in my hip muscle so smooth and easy that I hardly felt the stick over the pain in my head and shoulder.

"What are you giving him?" Conrad asked.

My heart softened knowing he cared about me.

"A tetanus shot and an antibiotic for any infection. His leg is hot to the touch and I'm afraid a fever is settling in." Doc Riley dropped the used syringes into a special red plastic container labeled "sharps."

By this time my eyes had adjusted to the barn lighting, and I saw a pretty gray dappled mare leaning her head on the stall gate watching me with big brown eyes.

I met her gaze.

Shyly, she looked away, lowered her head and limped from the gate. That's when I saw that her left leg was bandaged. That mare looked so sad, I felt sorrier for her than I did for myself. What was her name? What had happened to her?

"Conrad," the vet said. "I have to give Gunpowder a shot in his shoulder to numb the pain before I can sew up the wound."

This was the part that I was dreading, but I liked the idea of taking away the pain. The shot did hurt a little in my sore shoulder, but it wasn't too bad. I gritted my teeth, steeled my spine, and made it through.

Doc Riley placed reading glasses on the tip of his long slender nose, so he could see to thread the needle. "There it is," he murmured and hit the eye of the needle on the first try.

His steady hand went to work weaving the thread through the edges of the wound, drawing the two sides together, and pulling it tight, but not too tightly. He left a little room for the

17

wound to drain. After giving me twelve beautiful stitches, he tied the end to keep it from coming undone.

Doc Riley spoke to Conrad who'd been watching all this time. "I'll leave him stitched up until the skin begins to close on its own. I'll have to say, that's one of the best sewing jobs I've done in a while."

"Thanks, Doc." Conrad looked relieved, and readjusted his cowboy hat. "He's gonna be okay?"

"He'll make a full recovery."

"Can we take him home?"

Doc Riley scratched his whiskers. "I want to keep Gunpowder here for a few days for observation and give him more antibiotics."

Huh? Me? Spend the night? At the vet? I don't mind telling you that shook me up. I hadn't spent the night away from Conrad since he bought me at the Brownwood horse auction two years ago.

"Don't you think he would be better at home in his own barn?" Conrad bit his bottom lip. Shifted his weight. Stuck his hands in his pocket. Took them out again.

Yes. Good question.

"Son, I promise to have him back home as soon as possible." Doc Riley rested a hand on Conrad's shoulder. "Don't worry. He should be just fine. I'll let you say your goodbyes."

Conrad led me into the stall next to the mare and removed my halter, "Don't worry, buddy," he whispered. "Doc Riley is gonna take good care of you."

I was homesick already, and it was all I could do not to cry. I didn't want to stay here by myself.

He rubbed my nose and gently patted my good shoulder. He checked my water bucket and hay bin to make sure they were full. "I'll come see you tomorrow."

Please don't go.

With a small sad wave, he followed Herman and Mr. Winks out of the barn. Doc Riley followed, shutting off the lights.

Things went cold, still, and dark. In the stall next to me, I heard hay falling from the bin, and the soft sound of munching.

That was right, I'd almost forgotten about the mare. "Excuse me, mare. If it's not too rude of a question, what happened to your leg?"

"Bad accident with some old rusty barbed wire," she said.

Rusty barbed wire is the devil to a horse. It blends in with the dirt and by the time you see it, it's usually too late. Sometimes I wonder if the inventor of barbed wire gave a thought to how it could hurt horses. I haven't been cut by barbed wire yet, but I've had several near misses.

"I'm sorry to hear that," I said. "I had a run in with a mean old tiger-striped cow."

"Ouch," the mare said. "You must have been very brave."

That comment had me liking her a lot. "Name's Gunpowder. What's yours?"

"I'm Ladybug."

"How long have you been here, Ladybug?"

"Got here last night."

"Where you from," I asked, trying to spark up more conversation.

"Gentry Stables."

I'd heard about the place. Fancy riding stables where they catered to city folks who wanted to learn how to ride horses.

"Do you like it there?" I asked.

"I love it." Her voice was wistful. "I work as a therapy horse to help children heal from trauma and illness."

"Sounds rewarding."

"It's such a joy. I miss my owner, and I can't wait to go home."

"Me either," I said. We had something in common.

She shifted, and even in the darkness, I could see her wince.

I smiled kindly at her. "I can see you don't feel well, so I'll shut up and let you get some rest."

"Thank you, Gunpowder. Maybe I'll feel more like talking in the morning."

"Sleep well."

"You too."

Normally, I enjoy night time when all the livestock are fed, and the dry Texas air cooled off. My muscles would ache from a long day of riding, working cattle, or racing Conrad's friends on their horses after Cowboy School. But it was a good kind of achy. Not like this pain.

But this place was strange and smelled like medicine, and I was missing the Mesquite Bean Ranch. Here I was all stitched up and sore, not from doing all those fun things, but because some crazy cow thought we were going to hurt her baby.

I tossed and turned, trying to get comfortable and finally fell asleep.

A bad dream woke me up a couple of hours later. I was in a cold sweat. I'd dreamed the cow had gotten hold of Conrad. I couldn't save him. I just stood there and watched the cow maul him as he screamed. What a nightmare! My head had quit throbbing, but my shoulder was on fire.

I tried rolling over onto my good shoulder and go back to sleep, but it hurt too. I'd probably bruised it when I crashed into the tree after the cow and I collided.

Sunrise couldn't come soon enough.

"Ladybug?" I whispered. "You awake?"

She didn't answer, so I kept quiet. At least someone was getting some rest.

After a few more hours the morning light came creeping in through the windows and I let out a sigh of relief. At last. I peeked over into Ladybug's stall, but she was still asleep.

"Hey, newbie!" someone said.

Puzzled, I looked around, saw no one. "Where are you?"

"Out here."

I poked my head over the stall gate and looked down.

There stood a big red and white goat with big horns that curved straight back but didn't curl.

"Who are you?" I asked.

"Hi, I'm Strawberry, the vet clinic goat. My job is to welcome all new animals and answer any questions you might have."

"How'd you get that job?" I asked, grateful to have something to think about besides the pain.

"I came in one day for a small surgery on parts that I'd rather not mention." Strawberry looked a little embarrassed. "My owner didn't come back for me."

A scary feeling ran down my withers. What kind of owner didn't come back for his animal? And then a scared voice at the back of my mind whispered, *What if Conrad didn't come back for you?*

"Why not?" I asked.

"Don't know for sure. I'm guessing the surgery cost more money than he had."

"So he just left you?" In my head, I was trying to figure out how much it was going to cost for being here, and how Herman was going to pay for it.

The goat shrugged like he didn't care, but I caught a glimpse of sadness in his big teary eyes. "Hey, it happens."

"I'm sorry about that," I mumbled, my throat tightening as I tried to imagine what it would be like to be abandoned by my owner.

"It all turned out for the best. Doc Riley decided to keep me. He said that he needed a good therapy goat to keep the stressed horses company." Strawberry puffed out his chest like he was real proud of that.

"How'd you get your name?"

"One day Doc Riley caught me drinking some strawberry soda that someone left sitting on the ground by the wash rack. I drank up what I spilled over on the concrete, and even licked up what I could out of the bottle. It was sweet and fruity. And since I'm red and sweet, he named me Strawberry."

"That's really nice, Strawberry. My name is—"

"Gunpowder. Your owner is the little cowboy Conrad, and you live on the Mesquite Bean Ranch."

"Whoa there, my new goat friend. How do you know so much about me?"

Strawberry cocked his head. "Let's just say I don't miss much."

I cocked my head too. "Oh, I see, you're a nosy gossip."

He gasped. "I'm offended. I'm not a gossip. I just share information."

"Oh, calm down, Strawberry, I'm just digging you a little, don't be so sensitive."

"I'm not sensitive, I'm..."

Bark! Bark! Bark! Bark! Bark! Bark!

I swiveled my head around, saw a runaway horse being chased by a big collie dog. "Look out, Strawberry!"

The goat didn't even bother glancing around. "Oh, that's Doc Riley's ranch horse, Buck. I call him Houdini because that rascal can get out of any stall, pen, or pasture. He has a way of opening the gate with his top lip."

"Wow," I said, wishing I knew how to open the gate with my top lip. It sounded like a cool talent.

"Every time Buck gets out, Doc Riley's wife's collie dog goes to chasing him and barking and making a huge nuisance."

Yeah, I could hear that.

"Those two stir up all the sick dogs in the kennel, and everyone starts barking and howling. That sets off the sick cats, and they scream like broken fiddles. It takes me a good hour to get everyone to settle down. It's a challenge for my therapy skills."

I watched the horse trying to outrun the collie. "Wait, I think I know that horse."

"You do, Gunpowder. Along with Mr. Winks and Roany, you and Conrad helped work cattle with Doc Riley and Buck once."

The goat was right. I remembered Buck now. He was a decent sort, and I liked him. "How do you know all this stuff?"

"Buck is quite a storyteller, and he told me how you and Conrad pulled Mr. Winks and Roany out of a gully when Roany got flipped on his back."

"Hahaha, I'm so glad that story is making it around." I didn't want grouchy Roany to forget about that. It really got his gizzard. "So, how do I get to talk to Buck? I would love to tell him more choice stories about Roany."

"After Doc Riley catches him, he will put him back in the corral and tie the collie up. But by tonight it's possible Buck will be out again to roam."

Just then a young, dark-haired man strolled into the barn. "Welcome to the vet clinic, Gunpowder," he said with a Spanish accent. He poured a heaping scoop of food into my feed bucket. "Since you are my friend's cowpony, I will give you extra oats for breakfast."

"Did he say he was Conrad's friend?" I asked Strawberry. "I don't recognize him."

Strawberry rolled his big glazed eyes up at me. "Yeah, that's Juan. He and his family moved into the area a week ago. He works for Doc Riley on the weekends. I think he has been to Cowboy School just once or twice, so you may not have seen him yet. I like Juan. He's friendly, works hard, and he loves animals"

Juan leaned against my stall. "I heard about the wild cow that horned you. Poor guy, you must be really sore. But don't worry, I'll check on you and tell Conrad everything at school."

I bobbed my head and gave a gentle neigh in thanks. But, I knew that Conrad would be at the clinic soon to check on me. He was probably on his way right now. I just knew he'd missed me as much as I'd missed him.

CHAPTER THREE

THE OTHER HORSE

I patiently waited until noon, but no Conrad.

Doc Riley had given me more shots, one for the pain and another antibiotic. Juan led me to the wash rack to clean my wound, apply more dressing, and check on the stitches.

When I was back in my stall, Strawberry popped by.

"Hey, Gunpowder, did you see that mangy old cat that some lady just brought in?"

"I guess I missed him. What was special about him?"

"His hair was so knotted, and he looked like he hadn't eaten much but grasshoppers and frogs for a month. My guess, he's not much of a mouser. I bet the lady that brought him in didn't take good care of him at all!"

"Strawberry, is that all you have time to do?"

"What do you mean, Gunpowder?"

"I mean, you have no idea what the situation is on that

cat. Heck, the lady could have picked him up on the side of the road and felt sorry for him. You need to quit being such a gossip."

"I'm gonna ignore that." Strawberry tossed his head. "Since you're feeling bad 'cause your boy hasn't shown up yet, and you're taking it out on me."

Was I?

Clink, clank, bang. Herman's pickup rattled as it pulled into the parking lot of the vet clinic.

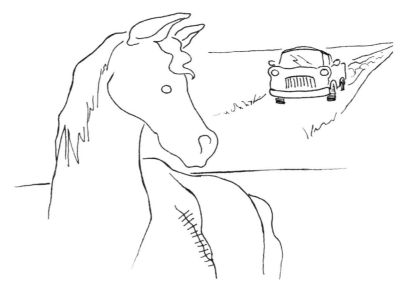

That sound was music to my ears. It meant my little buddy was coming to see me. "Ha," I told Strawberry. "Conrad's here."

A few minutes later, Herman got out of the pickup and strolled into the barn. Conrad's mom, Anne, was not far behind.

"Howdy, Gunpowder," Herman said.

"Hello, sweet cowpony." Anne rubbed my back and nose. "You saved our little boy."

"Hello, ma'am!" Juan, who'd been mucking out the stalls, waved at me. "Gunpowder is doing just fine. Doc Riley fixed him right up, and I'm making sure he has feed, hay, and water."

"Thank you, Juan," she said.

"Is Conrad with you?"

"No." Anne shook her head. "Conrad was too busy to come with us."

Conrad too busy? For me? I felt my jaws flush and my stomach twinge. A little knot of sadness growing big fast.

Strawberry smirked at me.

"Wait just a short minute, Strawberry. My boy is just as honorable and good as you've heard and I'm sure there must be a good reason for him not coming."

"Yeah, he's too busy for you."

"Oh yeah, that's right. It *is* the weekend. Saturday and Sunday mornings are prime calf working time, and I bet he is helping Mr. Winks and the other ranch hands round up those baby calves. He can't miss that."

"Hmm," said Strawberry. "If you're here, who's your boy riding this morning?"

That little knot in my stomach grew to the size of a boulder.

Strawberry made a good point. If Conrad was working cattle this morning, who was he working them with?

At the thought of Conrad on another horse, my heart tore right in two. One thing was for sure. I needed to get well, and fast. Before my boy replaced me for good.

Juan made evening rounds, cleaning the stalls, and feeding the animals. My appetite wasn't the best, and I wasn't sure if it was because of my injury or from being forgotten by Conrad. Or, the idea of my boy riding some other horse besides me.

I finished my bucket of oats, took a long drink of water, and laid down on the nice thick layer of fresh pine shavings and drifted off to sleep.

"Hey, Lazy Bones, have you been sleeping all day or what?"

Huh? Was I dreaming or was that Conrad's voice?

"Hey, Gunpowder, wake up, buddy, wake up."

I opened my eyes.

Conrad stood at the stall gate. The sun was just going down behind him. In the light from the setting sun, all I could make out was his silhouette.

My heart leaped. He was here. He'd come. He hadn't forgotten me after all.

"Can you get up?" He sounded worried.

My shoulder hurt the most when I got up from lying down. But I didn't want Conrad to fret. I gritted my teeth and held in a grunt as I pushed up.

I walked to the stall gate and put my head up so he could give me a good rub between the eyes and ears like he always does. He rubbed me extra gentle knowing that I took a big hit on the head.

"That's gonna leave a really cool scar on your shoulder. You were already the coolest cowpony at Cowboy School, but now you have a war wound to make you extra cool."

I nuzzled his shoulder. I didn't care about cool. All I cared about was Conrad. Seeing him made everything better.

"Now you and Scarbutt can compare scars," he said, talking about a mare I was friends with at Cowboy School. "I told everyone about how you saved me from getting hooked and stomped and tossed around by that tiger-striped cow. You're a local hero, Gunpowder."

Maggie and Tuffy came loping through the open barn door. I peeked around the side of the stall to see Mr. Winks truck and trailer rig sitting in the parking lot.

"Maggie! Tuffy!" hollered Mr. Winks as he came into view, spurs jangling and hands waving. "Get back in the pickup you two pot licking hounds."

The dogs paid him no mind. Instead, they ran over to Juan who was stacking hay at the back of the barn. Juan knelt down to pet them, and all excited, they licked his face.

"*Que pasa*, Juan?" Mr. Winks said, asking him 'what was up' in Spanish.

Juan grinned like sunshine. "*Trabajo, Señor Winks, trabajo.*"

For those who don't know, *trabajo* means "work" in Spanish.

"You are a heck of a worker, Juan. If you ever want to make some extra money, just say the word. We can always use a good cowhand at Mesquite Bean Ranch."

"Hey, I'm all the help you need at the ranch," Conrad protested and looked worried.

I knew how he felt. I was worried too; about that new

horse he'd been riding.

"You're my best cowboy, Conrad," Mr. Winks said, "But you've only got two hands. We'll need all the help we can get when we start building fences and hauling hay."

"Oh, ya…yea…yeah, I guess you're right about that," Conrad stuttered.

"Don't worry," Mr. Winks said. "No one is going to replace you."

I wished I could say the same thing.

As if picking up on my gloomy mood, Conrad gently massaged my neck. "Boy, Gunpowder, we sure could have used you today."

Pricking up my ears, I stretched closer to him. What had I missed out on?

"We took Maggie, Tuffy, Roany, and the bay and went looking for that devil cow that hooked you."

We? Who had Conrad been riding? My wound throbbed, and I felt kind of sick to my stomach. I blew out air, cooling my bottom lip.

"We looked all over the ranch and even into the neighbor's pasture, but we came up empty," Conrad went on.

Was this other horse in *my* corral? Was he eating *my* oats and hay? Was he drinking from *my* water trough?

Mr. Winks leaned against the stall gate. "That cow's got a calf hidden. Maybe in one of the thickets, and we can't get in there."

I could get in there. If I wasn't hurt.

"She could have hidden her calf in one of the canyon breaks," Conrad mused.

Mr. Winks nodded. "Yep. She's a fence jumper, roaming from ranch to ranch, looking for the best grass."

I felt itchy and restless. I hated that they were going out looking for the calf without me.

"We had a hard day of riding, and we'll get another tomorrow, but don't worry about me," Conrad said. "The bay horse I'm riding is sure footed and tough."

Bay? Who was this mysterious bay?

"That's right." Mr. Wink's adjusted his cowboy hat. "We won't quit until we find that ornery cow and her calf and get them roped up and off the ranch. After what she did to you, Gunpowder, she's too dangerous to have around."

Doc Riley appeared, limping down the shed row of the barn.

"What happened to you, Doc? Why are you limping?" Mr. Winks asked.

"Darned ol' mule stepped on my foot while I was trying to dislodge a bad mesquite thorn out of his shoulder. It'll be fine, just a bruise," Doc Riley grumbled.

"You sure?" Mr. Winks lifted his cowboy hat and scratched the top of his head.

"Forget about me. That's one good looking bay you got in your trailer standing next to Roany. Can you get him out, so I can have a closer look?"

"You bet we can," Mr. Winks said in a too-loud voice.

Oh no! They were going to trot that upstart bay right out in front of me? My stomach soured, and I wished I hadn't eaten so many oats.

"His name is Ringo," Mr. Winks said. "And he sure is a beauty."

Hmph. Beauty wasn't very useful in a cow horse. Much better to be quick and agile and brave like me.

Doc Riley, Juan, Conrad, Strawberry, and I watched as Mr. Winks sauntered out to the trailer. I had to crane my neck around the side of my stall to get a good look.

Mr. Winks opened the trailer gate and unloaded the bay.

The wind kicked up at just that time and feathered the bay's long silky mane down his back as he trotted into the barn.

As bad as I hate to admit it, the bay was one fantastic looking piece of horseflesh. He was a rich bay color with four black legs from the knees down, black mane and tail, and black coloring around his head.

The bay stepped lively as Mr. Winks paraded him around the barn for Doc Riley to get a better look. His powerful shoulders and hips made his steps so light, and he moved with such confidence, I wasn't sure his hooves even touched the ground.

Uh-oh. I got a sinking feeling inside me, almost as bad as when I spotted that tiger-striped cow.

Conrad's eyes glistened, and his voice rose with excitement. "We rode in some pretty rough country this morning, but Ringo doesn't miss a step."

Juan whistled. "He is something."

Ringo tossed his head, sent his flowing mane shaking and smirked at me.

That just about did it, I couldn't take much more. I whinnied so loud I thought my eyes would bulge out of my head.

But Conrad just kept right on talking about that bay. "Doc Riley, I had to rope a steer on him this morning, and he handled the rope and the steer superbly."

His words were a knife to my heart. What in the world was Conrad doing, doting over this new horse?

I snorted, wheeled around and kicked the stall gate hoping to get Conrad's attention off the bay and onto me. But all I got was a snarly glare from Doc Riley. "Stop that."

That kicking stirred up the pain in my shoulder. Not smart.

"Well, Conrad," Doc Riley said. "Ringo sure is a nice horse. Best keep him away from that mean tiger-striped cow and her calf."

"Yes, sir."

"I'll do what I can for your other horse."

Did Doc Riley just call me the "other" horse? As if I didn't have a name? As if I didn't matter?

"You mean, Gunpowder," said Conrad.

That made me feel a little bit better, but not much. That Ringo was still flouncing around like he was king of the corral.

"When do you think Gunpowder will be ready to come back to the Mesquite Bean Ranch?" Mr. Winks asked the vet.

"It'll be a few days. I'll let you know. Heck, Conrad, you sure won't be afoot while your other horse heals up. You'll be riding that fine, handsome bay."

Mr. Winks walked Ringo past me on the way back to the trailer.

That bay cocked his head, gave a smart aleck sidelong look and an eerie smile at me that sent shivers to my tail. That dude was bad news, and I couldn't say anything to anybody to prove it. I just had a really bad feeling.

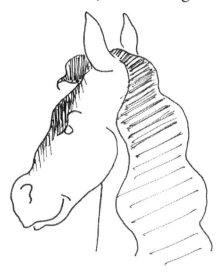

And it wasn't because I was jealous. Okay, yes, I *was* jealous, but this feeling wasn't about that. Something about Ringo the bay was definitely not right.

I wanted to load up in the trailer and squeeze Ringo out. But, the harder I pressed on the stall gate with my shoulder, the more it burned. This healing was going to take entirely too long. I had to get out of here, and make sure the bay didn't take over my boy.

"Load up, dogs," Mr. Winks called to Tuffy and Maggie, and they hopped into the back of the truck.

"Well, Gunpowder," Conrad said, sad but not as sad as last night. "It's getting late and we need to get the horses back to the ranch and get some oats in their bellies. I promise to come by earlier tomorrow. Hopefully, you'll be home soon, buddy."

Take me home now, I'm all better.

I tossed my head to show him how good I was doing, and a searing pain shot through my shoulders.

Maybe not as good as I hoped.

Conrad hugged me around the neck, told me goodnight, and then he was gone. Off with that pretty-boy bay.

"It's okay, *compadre*," Juan said, picking up on my sadness. *Compadre* means "friend" in Spanish, and I liked that he considered me a friend. "You will be well in no time. And, back where you belong."

I bounced my nose in agreement.

Juan gave me some extra oats, and gently rubbed my head between my eyes before he said, "goodnight" and went home.

I appreciated Juan being nice with the oats and rubbing, but I didn't have much appetite. No matter how hard I tried,

I couldn't stop thinking about Ringo.

I felt restless and edgy. Sometimes pacing helped to clear my mind, but I couldn't even pace back and forth in the stall because my dang shoulder hurt so bad. I really wished Doc Riley would come by and give me something for the pain. But he didn't.

Bright moonlight radiated through the barn allowing me to see everything pretty well. I felt the stitches stretch every time I got up or laid down in the stall. I felt like an old grandpa horse, getting around so slowly.

Feeling sorry for myself, worrisome thoughts circled around in my head. Was there a chance that Ringo could knock me out of the picture? What if I didn't heal right? What if he was a faster, better cowpony? What if Conrad liked him more than me?

Okay, okay, Gunpowder, get a hold of yourself. Conrad loves you.

To distract myself, I poked my head over the gate to see if that pesky goat Strawberry was hanging around for a bit of gossip about Ringo, but there was no sight of him.

I whinnied for Strawberry at the top of my lungs. The dogs in the kennel howled and the sick cats meowed.

"What's all the commotion?" asked Ladybug from the next stall.

"I'm looking for Strawberry the goat. Have you seen him? I need to ask him some questions. I bet he's over in the cow lot, eavesdropping on conversations."

"I don't know where he is, but maybe I can help," Ladybug said.

"Did you see that handsome bay that was here this evening? Goes by the name of Ringo. I need to know who he is."

"No, I'm sorry, Gunpowder. Doc Riley had me inside the clinic doing x-rays on my cut leg, but maybe Buck knows him." Ladybug whinnied in a real pretty female horse language that would get Buck's attention if anything would.

A few minutes later Buck came jogging around the corner into the vet barn, stirring up dust in the moonlight. "You called, little mare?"

She fluttered her eyelashes. "Why, yes I did. Gunpowder needs to know about a bay horse named Ringo."

"Buck, how do you get out so easy?" I asked.

"It's not hard. Just take your top lip and flip the handle up on the latch. But you have to catch it with your bottom lip before it locks back down. Then slide the lever over, push the gate with your chest and voilà. You're out."

"How come Doc Riley doesn't put a better latch on your pen?"

"He doesn't care if I get out and roam around as long as I don't go too far. I also have Mrs. Riley's collie dog watching my every move. But she's out chasing bunnies right now."

"Back to Ringo," I said. "What do you know about him?"

Buck popped his bottom lip and raised an eyebrow. "That bay belongs to Mr. Mason, owner of the biggest ranch in the county."

I knew who Mr. Mason was. Conrad and I had a few run-ins with his boys when we first started Cowboy School. The Mason name left a bad taste in my mouth.

"Yep, ol' Ringo is one of many horses of the Mason Ranch

remuda."

"What's a remuda?" I asked.

"Big ranches have herds of horses that aren't regularly used like us. Second string horses, if you will."

"That's gotta be rough. Not having a regular place to stay."

"Don't feel too sorry. They're second sting because they usually have a bad habit or two. Which is why they don't get to live at ranch headquarters. They are turned out with the herd and only brought in when needed. They don't get fresh grain every day or have a good barn to get out of the weather."

Boy, I sure was glad I wasn't a second-string horse. "So, they are sort of like outlaws?"

Buck laughed. "Never thought of it that way, but yeah."

"What kind of bad habit do you think Ringo has?"

"The only thing I've seen so far working cattle with him is that he spooks and shies away really quick."

"Does that mean his rider would get left in the dirt if Ringo is put in a bind?"

Buck bobbed his head. "I'm sure Ringo wouldn't have stayed to fight the tiger-striped cow like you did."

That made me feel good. "Why do you think Mr. Winks is letting my little owner ride him?"

Buck chuffed. "Ringo looks pretty and he moves with such ease. He's big and stout and can probably pull as much as I can. He's also smart…maybe too smart."

"Come to think of it…." Buck sized me up. "Ringo kind of looks like you, Gunpowder. He's a bay same as you and even has the same dark legs, mane, and tail. Hmm, that's funny."

There was absolutely nothing at all that was funny about my Conrad riding another cowpony that looked like me. I had to get healed up, back to the ranch, and get that Ringo out of the picture…*pronto!*

CHAPTER FOUR

FAKE IT, TILL YOU MAKE IT

The next morning, after Juan had fed me a big scoop of oats, I heard Doc Riley holler, "Juan, get Ladybug ready, she's going home soon."

That put a little jingle in my jangle! If Ladybug was headed home already, surely it wouldn't be long before I would head home too.

Strawberry shook the flies off his ears. "Baaaaa! I like to see patients being dismissed because it means I've done my job."

"What? Do you think you had something to do with healing her?"

"Sure, my stories perked her right up."

I rolled my eyes. "Whatever makes you feel important, Strawberry."

"Wonder if you will have to share your corral with Ringo

41

when you go home?" He gave a sly grin.

I looked down at him and in a calm, low voice, and I said, "Strawberry, there's no need to be a smart aleck."

He shook his horns again, "I bet your boy and his new horse will be hanging out at Cowboy School come Monday."

Good grief, I hadn't thought of Ringo going to Cowboy School with Conrad.

Would Ringo wear my saddle and blankets? Was he standing in *my* corral talking with *my* friends, Scarbutt and Chief? Would he make up who-knows-what kind of stories about me?

Around mid-day a shiny red pickup pulling an empty, white, two-horse trailer pulled into the parking lot of the vet clinic. The trailer looked new, and the pickup didn't rattle or bang.

An older lady stepped out, holding a pretty nylon green halter and a white cotton lead rope coiled in her hand.

Juan hurried over to her. "Good morning, ma'am. Are you here to pick up Ladybug?"

"Yes, I am," she said in a gentle voice. "I'm here to take her home."

"Yes, ma'am, I'll get her right away." Juan accepted the halter and lead rope from the woman.

"Ladybug," I said to the mare who was sticking her head out of the stall next to me. "I guess this is your ride."

"Yes, that's my owner, and I'm so ready to go home."

"I'm happy for you," I said, and meant it, but I was sad for me too. The barn would be lonelier without her.

"Gunpowder, try not to worry too much," she said. "You will heal quickly and be back with your boy soon."

"That's kind of you to say. I'll miss you."

"I'll miss you too."

"Watch out for that barbed wire." I got a catch in my throat.

"Thanks." She lowered her lashes at me. "I will."

She was limping when Juan led her from the stall, but as soon as she saw the woman, Ladybug perked up and started prancing.

Wow, was she feigning feeling better just to get to go home sooner? Had she somehow bamboozled Doc Riley into letting her leave early?

"Hey, Ladybug," I called. "What are you up to?"

She lowered her lashes at me, neighed softly. "Faking it until I make it."

Hmm, maybe I should try that trick?

I want to be very clear that I don't like being deceitful, but I was desperate, and desperate times call for desperate action.

43

I had to get home and get rid of Ringo.

Strawberry must have seen a devious glimmer in my eye. "I guess you'll be faking it now?"

I looked at that goat sternly in the eye. "Don't say a word! I'm not proud, but a horse has to do, what a horse has to do."

"And, what is that?" Strawberry asked.

"I have to get back to the ranch, and make sure that Ringo hasn't already permanently taken a place under *my* saddle blanket."

"What if you end up getting hurt even more by pretending to be healing better than you are?"

I tossed my head with confidence. "Won't happen?"

"It's only worth being cocky if you can back it up. Be careful, Gunpowder."

"Thanks for looking out for me, Strawberry. But I know what I'm doing."

"Okay," Strawberry said. "Just know if things go wrong, it could will be the end of your cowpony career."

U *U* *U*

At noon, Herman, Anne, and Conrad came by to visit after church, but they couldn't stay long. More work to do around the ranch. And Conrad was still yapping about how great Ringo was.

On Monday, Juan took me to the wash rack, at Doc Riley's instruction, and pressure washed my cut. The cold water numbed the cut and cleaned out the infection.

That little procedure was unpleasant to say the least, but I gritted my teeth and did my best to show it was healing and not painful.

Taking a cue from Ladybug, I knew I had to make this believable, so that Doc Riley would let me go home.

A few minutes later, Doc Riley came into the barn to examine my wound. He made approving noises and nodded his head. "Juan, please walk Gunpowder down to his stall and back, so I can see if he's still limps."

This was it. *Showtime.* I had to make sure this walk went off without a hitch.

Juan clicked his tongue, led me to the stall.

Gingerly, I set my right hoof on the ground. It was so numb, that I couldn't feel the dirt. I had to be careful. With the numbness in my hoof, I could easily sprain my fetlock, which is like an ankle on a human.

It was no easy task to put pressure on a numb hoof without limping.

The first step was a bit wobbly, but by paying close attention, I was able to walk to the stall and back without the slightest sign of a limp.

With each twinge of pain, I would take a deep breath and think of Conrad going for a joy ride on Ringo.

After I put on my show, Doc. Riley rubbed his chin. "Juan, I think Gunpowder is ready. He'll be going home tomorrow."

Yay! I let out a deep breath. I'd done it. I'd faked out Doc Riley. But in doing so, would Strawberry's ominous words come back to haunt me?

If things go wrong, it could be the end of your cowpony career.

♘ ♘ ♘

Rattle, bark, bang. Rattle, bark, bang. The sound of Mr. Winks' ranch pickup and trailer bouncing down the caliche county road to the vet clinic the next morning was music to my ears.

I knew it was Mr. Winks' rig because while Herman's pickup had similar rattles and bangs, there was no barking in between. The barking came from…you guessed right… Maggie and Tuffy. As annoying as those two dogs could be, they were a pleasant sight for sore eyes.

"Tuffy, stay in the pickup," Mr. Winks hollered. Maggie was such an obedient girl she knew not to get out. But Tuffy was a little on the hardheaded side and had to be told every time. Mr. Winks strolled into the barn where Juan was hosing the wash station clean.

"*Hola*, Mr. Winks," Juan greeted him and turned off the water hose.

"Howdy, Juan. Can you get Gunpowder ready for me while I speak to Doc Riley about a sick cow that I've been doctoring at the ranch?"

"That's okay, Mr. Winks. I will load him for you."

Juan put the halter on me and led me to the trailer where Roany was waiting. Juan opened the gate and guided me up. Tuffy jumped out of the back of the pickup and came to sniff me in greeting.

I let a little grunt against the pain in my shoulder as I stepped inside.

"How long you gonna limp around on that little cut?" Roany asked.

"Dang, Roany," I said cheerfully, hoping Juan didn't notice that I'd been limping. "Are you naturally grumpy or do you have to work at it?"

Mr. Winks wandered out of the clinic, and pulled the brim of his cowboy hat down to block the sun. "Load up, Tuffy. I told you to stay!"

Tuffy ducked his head and ran back to the pickup.

"Thank you, Juan." Mr. Winks smiled.

"*De nada, Señor Winks*." Juan bobbed his head and gave me one last rub between my eyes. "He is a good horse."

"That he is." Mr. Winks turned his attention to me. "Let's get you home, Gunpowder."

"Hey, Winks." Doc Riley ran out to the parking area. "I forgot to tell you that Gunpowder will need some light exercise every day, so those torn muscles heal properly, and they won't get knotted up."

"We can sure do that, Doc," Mr. Winks said.

"One more thing, don't let anyone ride him for at least a month. He's still got a lot of healing to do. I'll be out to the ranch to check on him in a few days." Doc Riley gave Mr. Winks a brown paper bag. "Here's some extra powders for pain. Just mix them in his feed every evening."

Did Doc Riley just say a month?

Oh no! That was way too long.

Yes, I might be going home, but in the end, I was no closer to reclaiming my place with Conrad than I was before. If he couldn't ride me for a whole month, that means he'd be riding that outlaw Ringo.

And I'll still be in second place.

Honk! Honk! Mr. Winks blared the horn as we drove by the general store. Conrad, and his friends, Cody, and the Weatherford girls stood on the front porch with soda pops in their hands, watching a couple of old cowboys play dominoes.

I whinnied as loud as I could.

Conrad swept off his cowboy hat, grinned big and waved at us. We would beat him home to the Mesquite Bean.

I saw Ringo tied to the hitching post, and I bared my teeth at him. He tossed his head like he didn't care.

Just as we pulled through the ranch gate, I heard a, "Yeehaw" from behind us. I craned my neck around.

Here came Conrad spurring Ringo as hard as he could run. They were galloping so fast, they almost beat us to the barn.

Let me pause the story for a minute to talk about running your horse to the barn. It's a big "don't. Do not do it!" Here's why. Running your horse to the barn can instill bad habits. It's kind of like a bug being drawn to the barn light at night. They just can't help it. Every horse wants to run to the barn. We are not stupid. We know it means the saddle comes off, and we get to rest. In the summer it's a cool bath, and then often a big scoop of feed. In the winter it's a warm blanket. So, rule of thumb: Don't ever run your horse to the barn, or they will get spoiled and want to do it every time.

"Your gonna catch the whole barn on fire with the steam coming out of your ears," Roany said.

"That horse truly is an outlaw," I muttered.

"Sure you're not just jealous?" Roany was gigging me, but his eyes were kind.

"Of that guy? Not likely."

"It's easy to be jealous when someone is better than us at something."

I glowered. "I'm not jealous. I'm worried he's going to get Conrad hurt."

"And I'm worried you're letting your anger get the better of you."

Was Roany right? Was I just jealous of Ringo?

A flicker of shame licked through my belly. Maybe I *was* a little jealous, but that didn't mean I was wrong about Ringo. That horse was nothing but trouble, and I aimed to prove it.

CHAPTER FIVE

WELCOME BACK?

The next morning my shoulder was extra stiff and sore. I got up really slow and tried to stretch. Conrad came into the barn whistling; carrying our morning bucket of oats.

You know that feeling that you get when you think someone is staring at you? Well, I got it. The hairs on my neck tickled. I turned around to see Ringo giving me a hard stare and a sly smirk.

"Ringo, you better hurry and eat your oats, so we can get to school. We don't want to be late." Conrad came into my pen and started brushing me while I was eating. "How are you feeling this morning, buddy?"

I nudged the brim of his hat with my nose and popped my tail once to let him know that I missed him.

"You ready to go see the gang at Cowboy School?" He scratched my jaw.

I really was achy, but I wasn't about to limp. Fake it, till you make it, right? *Thanks for that tip, Ladybug.* I wanted to go to Cowboy School and see my friends. Plus, I wanted to be with Conrad every minute that I could, especially if Ringo was around.

Mr. Winks wandered into the barn with a cup of coffee in his hand. "Good morning, Conrad."

"Mornin', Mr. Winks."

"Do you need help with Gunpowder this morning? He seems really sore."

"He's probably just stiff from sleeping on the ground all night," Conrad said.

"Say, I have an idea, why don't you and Ringo go on to school? Roany and I will bring Gunpowder over around noon. I can feed him some pain powders and change his wound dressing, and you won't be late."

"Oh, that would be great. Thanks, Mr. Winks. Thanks."

No!

I appreciated Mr. Wink's thoughtful concern, but I had to keep an eye on Ringo. I didn't trust that horse one little bit. What if a rabbit or deer jumped out of the brush on the way to school and he quickly shied away? Bucking Conrad off and leaving him hurt on the road? What if he chomped down on the bit and ran away? What if he wanted to knock Conrad off under a low hanging tree branch?

But I didn't have any say in the matter. Conrad and Ringo set off for school, leaving me behind.

Roany said, "They'll be all right between here and school. Not much for them to get into."

"Not much for a regular horse like us, but Ringo's an outlaw," I reminded him.

"I'll try to hurry Mr. Winks along, so you can get to Cowboy School."

"Thanks a lot, Roany. I didn't know you cared that much." I grinned. Roany acted tough, but inside he was a good guy.

"Hey, don't push it young'un, or you'll push all the good out of my good will."

Mr. Winks gave me some pain medicine, poured cool water on my cut, put ointment on it, and then bandaged the wound. "The cut is healing well."

That's good. Maybe I was starting to "make it," and I wouldn't have to "fake it" much longer.

Mr. Winks put a halter and lead rope on me. Then took me to the tack room for a quick brushing. "Now you're ready for school."

I loved the short ride between the ranch and Cowboy School. I'd been cooped up for too long. We passed the small house where Herman, Anne, and Conrad lived. This time of day, nobody was home.

Anne had planted a fall garden, and she had clothes hanging out on the line to dry. The yard was mowed and well kept.

The place looked peaceful, and my old friend Seven, the milk cow, was eating hay behind a small barn. My heart lifted at the sight of her.

"Mooo!" she called.

I gave her a head bob and neighed back. "Hello, old friend."

"I hear you got hurt," she said following along on the inside of the fence as we passed by on the road.

"It was just a scratch," I said.

"That's not what I heard. The Mason boys' horses were talking as they were headed to Cowboy School, and I caught a snippet of their conversation. They said you were a "has been" and Ringo was going to take your place, and they were going to help make sure of it."

What? Anger steamrolled right through me. Not at my friend Seven, but at those Mason boys' horses, Trip and Trap, and their mean gossip.

"Don't believe that for a second," I told Seven. "You know me. I bounce back like a ball."

"Balls don't bounce if they get a hole in them." Seven gazed at my shoulder wound.

"It's healing up."

She looked like she wanted to believe me. "Just take care of yourself, Gunpowder. After listening to Trip and Trap talk, I don't trust them for a minute."

"Me either, Seven," I muttered. "Me either."

U   U   U

It was lunch time when we got to Cowboy School. All the kids were in the chuck line waiting to get their grub. Or, they'd already been served and were sitting at tables under the awning, or shade trees around the schoolyard.

As we approached, someone yelled, "Gunpowder is here!"

Conrad and his friends, which included, Cody, Juan, and the Weatherford girls: Ashley, Emily, and Kady, ran over holding up a big sign written in colored markers. The sign read: *Welcome back, Gunpowder!*

The rest of the kids rushed over to greet us too.

What do you know? They missed me. A tingle of happiness worked its way through my belly and into my heart.

"Step back, kids." Mr. Barton and the rest of the teachers strolled over to pat and rub on me. Everyone was extra gentle around my cut.

I was soaking up the attention, and loving every bit of it. After those days at the vet barn, it felt good to be back where I belonged.

"Wow! That's a cool looking scar, Gunpowder," Cody said.

"You are a bona fide hero."

His kind words put a little starch in my tail, and I forgot about my aches and pains.

Conrad took the rope from Mr. Winks and led me toward the stable. "We have a nice pen with lots of fresh straw in it for you to lay down, and I put you in next to your friends, Scarbutt and Chief."

Scarbutt was Ashley Weatherford's horse and Chief belonged to Cody. They were both experienced cowponies, respected and admired by many younger horses in our ranching community. They respected me, too.

"I figured you and Scarbutt could trade war stories about your scars," Conrad said.

The Weatherford girls had followed us, and they hung up the welcome sign, strung with bailing wire, on the barn door where I could see it. They gave me more scratches and rubs, and all my troubles melted away.

Finally, the lunch was over, and the kids had to go to the classroom.

"We've been thinking about you, Gunpowder." Scarbutt batted her eyes. She sure was a pretty mare. Prettier even, than Ladybug.

"Thanks, Scarbutt," I smiled and lowered my head, feeling a little shy around her. "I guess you heard about that *devil* cow?"

"Oh yes, we've been waiting to hear your side of the tale." Scarbutt knew I was itching to tell the story, so she let on like she didn't know much.

Chief winked at Scarbutt. "Okay, Gunpowder, lay it on

us!"

They were all good friends. I launched into the story of how I fought off that brindle cow. I'm not gonna lie and say that I didn't exaggerate. Because I did. Just a little. Tall tales make better stories, right? I figured I have the wound, and that qualifies me to put a little extra molasses on the oats, if you know what I mean.

"Ahem…" said a voice from outside the other side of the barn. "That's not the way I heard the story."

I glanced over my shoulder to see…

Guess who?

Yep, it was Ringo and he was standing beside Levi and Randy Mason's paint horses, Trip and Trap.

Trip and Trap were just as mischievous as their owners. They thought they were prettier and sleeker than any horses in the country. I'm surprised they could walk ten yards without stumbling over their own ego.

After we left them in the dust in the annual Cowboy School calf roping competition last year, those two really hated me.

They made every excuse in the book to justify why they'd lost. Trip claimed his calf ran too hard for him to catch up. Trap said he'd gotten a slow one that didn't put up enough of a fight. Trip said he'd slipped in the roping box. Trap blamed it on a horsefly that kept biting his eyes. Both said that they'd done their part, but it was Randy and Levi that messed up on the roping.

Bottom line? Conrad and I won fair and square.

"It figures," I said curling my lip at Ringo.

"What does?" Ringo narrowed his eyes to slits.

"That you'd herd up with some of your own kind." I squared my jaw. "Birds of a feather flock together."

"You calling me names, Gunpowder?" Ringo looked at his two companions. "Y'all heard him call us birds, right?"

The other two horses bared their teeth at me.

I stuck my head over the stall gate, glared a hole through him. "Listen, Ringo, and listen good. If you turn cowardly and duck out from under Conrad, you'll have more trouble than you can handle."

Ringo smiled sly as a fox. "Why would I do that? You worry too much, Gunpowder."

I stared Ringo dead straight in the eye. "You are *not* Conrad's horse, and you never will be."

"Looks like I am to me," Ringo gloated. "Who's he riding now?" Then he tossed his mane and trotted off with the Mason horses.

Leaving me gritting my teeth and wondering just how in the world I was going to get rid of that Ringo.

So much for a fine welcome home.

The following morning Conrad hitched me to Ringo with a lead rope, and they guided me to school.

I don't mind telling you that I was none too happy to be trotting behind Ringo's backside. He sashayed his hips with an extra roll just to show off and let me know who was boss.

It took everything I had in me to keep up with his pace. My shoulder stung, and I had to take extra care where I placed my hoof because of that confounded numbness in my fetlock.

Somehow, I pulled it off because Mr. Barton was standing on the schoolhouse porch when we got there. "Hey, Conrad, Gunpowder sure is getting along nicely."

"Yes, sir, he is, Mr. Barton," Conrad climbed down off Ringo and untied the lead rope attaching me to that outlaw horse.

I sure was glad to be free of him.

"I bet in no time you'll be riding him again." Mr. Barton said.

That was music to soar my spirits.

Ringo backed his ears, curled his lip, bared his teeth, and shot me a look that said, *Not if I can help it.*

A shiver ran through my withers. Was he capable of violence? I didn't want to believe that, but I'd be dumb not to be leery of him. And, with Trip and Trap on his side, they were a triple threat.

Conrad led me and Ringo to the stables. We had to walk side by side.

I tensed, scared Ringo might lean over and nip my wounded shoulder. I wouldn't put it past him. I stayed as far away from him as the length of rope would allow.

Ringo snickered and bit the air, toying with me. I tried not to flinch, but I couldn't help it. All I could think of was his teeth biting into my wounded flesh.

The Mason boys, Randy and Levi, were astride Trip and Trap and blocking the stable entrance. Ringo smiled and swished his tail at Trip and Trap as if telling them "well done" for standing in our way.

Then when Conrad looked over at Ringo, he lowered his head, softened his eyes and put his ears forward, looking innocent, as if he didn't have a hand…or, hoof…in this.

"Could you guys please let us by?" Conrad asked nicely, but I could feel him tensing up on the rope.

"There's plenty of room to let one horse by us," Levi said.

"Yeah, there wouldn't be a problem," Randy chimed in. "If you'd leave that crippled horse at home. Everybody is tired of him taking up good space in the stable."

"Oh, really? Who is everybody? You and your brother?" Conrad fired back, tucking his thumbs through his belt loop and puffing out his chest. My little owner would fight anyone for me, just as I would fight anyone for him.

Conrad was still holding onto the ropes, so his gesture pulled me and Ringo closer together.

Ugh. I kept a sidelong glance pinned on Ringo, ready to bite first if he tried anything funny.

"Gunpowder sure ain't botherin' me." Cody came up behind us on foot. Cody was smiling like always, but there was a *Don't-tread-on-me-or-my-friends* gleam in his green eyes.

If there was one person in all of Cowboy School that could quell those ornery Mason boys, it was Cody. Mostly out of pure respect. Even the Mason boys knew Cody was the best roper in the county. They wouldn't admit it, but they knew. Everyone in Cowboy School did.

The Mason boys didn't move, they just smirked, challenging Conrad and Cody.

"Let us by," Conrad said, putting force in his voice.

"Whatcha gonna do if we don't?" Randy taunted. "Go tattle to Mr. Barton?"

Cody doubled up his fists. "Come down off your horses and find out."

"Boys!" Mr. Barton hollered across the schoolyard. "Get

your horses stabled. It's time for class."

With a lazy twitch of his lips, Randy clicked his tongue and guided Trap out of the doorway. Levi followed on Trip.

They were giving in because they had to, but I had a bad feeling that this wasn't over. Not by a long shot.

CHAPTER SIX

RANCH SORTING

After reading, writing, and arithmetic was over for the day, Mr. Barton brought the students to the stables for their afternoon cowhand classes.

"Kids, before you get your horses ready, I want to give you the details of our upcoming competition."

A competition? My ears pricked up. I loved competing. But as soon as my spirits soared, they sagged. I was in no shape to compete in anything more strenuous than a bellyaching contest.

"The event will consist of herd sorting, or as it's sometimes called, ranch sorting," Mr. Barton went on. "This is a skill that ranchers use every year when they separate the calves from their mamas to wean them."

Dang. Sorting was my favorite kind of competition.

I got excited then. I loved sorting. It was one of my

favorite things to do on a ranch. A good sorter—whether it be cowpony or cowhand—is worth his or her weight in gold and earns respect from any rancher.

"During the competition, you'll have to sort as many cattle as you can in one minute."

"Wow." Cody adjusted his Stetson, pulling the brim down lower on his forehead. "You gotta be awfully quick to win this one."

"Scared you're too slow?" Randy Mason taunted.

"Heck no." Cody grinned. "Just feeling sorry for you, Molasses Mason."

Randy jutted his chin out. "Who you calling molasses?"

"Boys." Mr. Barton scowled. "Hush and pay attention."

Cody and Randy stared each other down as Mr. Barton went on. "Each steer will have a number painted on their hip. Ten steers in each herd."

"Only ten?" Randy mumbled. "I can sort ten in ten seconds.

Mr. Barton ignored that. "You'll each be given a number to start with, and you'll sort them out in sequential order."

Levi raised a hand. "Huh?"

"For example," Mr. Barton said. "If I tell you to sort the number five steer, you sort him first, then you sort number, six, seven and so on."

"Wait, what?" Randy scratched his head. "Why wouldn't you start with number one? The cowhand who starts with five will only get to herd up five steers."

"Six," Conrad corrected.

"Huh?" Randy pinched his face tight, looking like a weasel.

Conrad held up his fingers and counted them off. "Five, six, seven, eight, nine, ten."

Randy stuck out his tongue at Conrad.

"Knock it off, boys." Mr. Barton snapped his fingers. "Randy, if you start with number five, and you have time left to sort more cattle after you reach ten, then you'll go to number one, two, etcetera…"

Randy folded his arms. "I still don't know why you can't just start with number one."

"To keep you kids on your toes." Mr. Barton looked put out with Randy. "If you sort the steers out of order, your time stops."

"Even if it's not a full minute?" Levi whined.

"Even if it's not a full minute," Mr. Barton confirmed. "I will drop the flag to start the time and blow the whistle to end it."

"What if a horse bites or kicks a steer?" Conrad asked, giving the Mason boys a warning look, while I kept an eye on Trip and Trap. I wouldn't put anything past those two.

"If your horse bites or kicks the steers, you will be disqualified. Keep those ponies on their best behavior," Mr. Barton said. "Any other questions?"

Cody's arm shot into the air.

"Yes, Cody?"

"What's first prize if we win?" "

"Good question. The winner will receive thirty dollars and second place will get twenty. Third place gets a free soda at the general store." Mr. Barton rubbed his palms together. "Let's get a head count. Whoever wants to enter, please raise your hand."

Cody, Ashley, Conrad, Randy, Levi, and Juan all raised their hands. Cody would ride, Chief, Ashley on Scarbutt, Randy and Levi entered with Trip and Trap, and Juan would use his horse, Oso.

Oso means 'bear" in Spanish. I guess Juan named him that because Oso is big and brown like a grizzly bear.

And Conrad would pair with Ringo.

My heart dropped to my hooves. It made sense. Who else would he ride while I was laid up? I had no choice but to sit this one out. I rotated my sore shoulder. Ouch! Yep, not in competition shape. I had some unkindly thoughts about that devil cow who'd gotten me into this predicament.

The kids were grinning and jumping around and chattering nonstop. I wished I could share their excitement.

Cody said, "I'm not so sure that we'll do too good on this one. Chief is an awesome roping horse, but he's no spring chicken. Moving fast from side to side doesn't come easily to him anymore."

Chief looked over at me. "Sadly enough, he's right."

"Scarbutt can sure cut em out of the herd, but she gives every now and again on her scarred hip, so we'll see," Ashley said.

"Oso is so big and strong he can pull a barn but not too sure about sorting cattle." Juan shook his head.

Levi smarted off. "Our paints are the best in the county when it comes to any kind of ranch work, so y'all should just quit now. I'll get first and Randy will get second."

"Hush up, Levi!" Randy doubled up his fist and frogged

69

his little brother in the shoulder. "You have a big mouth, and by the way, I'll get first. Not you!"

Everyone looked at Conrad. He was the only one who hadn't spoken up.

He didn't say a word.

"What about you, Conrad?" asked Ashley.

Conrad looked over his shoulder at me in the pen and dropped his chin. "I'm not sure. Ringo is pretty quick, but I feel like I'm betraying Gunpowder. But, if I ride Ringo and win, I could use the money to pay off Gunpowder's vet bill."

I'm pretty sure both of my ears drooped at the same time. For the first time, I wondered if maybe all this was my fault. If I hadn't let Conrad vaccinate that calf, his angry mama wouldn't have charged us.

"Hey, Gunpowder, pick your head up! Trip and Trap are laughing at you. They love seeing you down and depressed," Chief said.

Chief was right. The paints and Ringo had formed a little gang and they would work to squeeze me out.

"Chief, why do you think Trip and Trap have thrown in with Ringo?" I asked.

Chief shrugged. "Who knows? I'm not sure what he's telling them, but I was wondering the same thing. I'll keep an ear out for you."

I couldn't even pick up my spirits and on the way home from school, I plodded behind Ringo with my head down. I felt guilty about that vet bill and sad over Ringo taking my place. I didn't even try not to limp. No more faking it until I made it. My heart wasn't in it.

When we reached Mesquite Bean Ranch, Conrad left me in the corral and went inside his house. He came back out in a few minutes with his father.

"What's wrong, son," Herman asked.

"I'm not sure, Dad. Gunpowder started limping, and he kept his head down all the way home from school."

Herman crouched to examine my wound. "Hmm? I wonder if his shoulder is bothering him. He's not completely healed yet, and we might have been pushing him too hard. Or, he could have a fever."

"I hope it's not a fever." Conrad chewed on his bottom lip.

You go ahead and unsaddle Ringo, and I'll look after

Gunpowder."

"Yes, sir."

Herman took my temperature. "No fever." He scratched my head between my ears. "If it's not a fever, what's got you so down, Gunpowder?"

I wished I could tell him that rascal Ringo had me feeling lower than a snake's belly in a wagon rut.

Herman picked up and cleaned out all four of my hooves. He ran his hand up and down my legs searching for signs of an infection. "No heat in your joints either. I'll be darned if I can see anything wrong."

I whinnied, and wished that I could speak human.

"Unless…you're feeling sad?" Herman eyed me. "Naw, that's plumb crazy. Horses don't get depressed."

I longed to tell him, *yes sir, yes we do.*

Herman led me to the stables, unsaddled me, combed me out and then went back to the house.

"You gonna mope around all evening feeling sorry for yourself?" Roany asked.

"I'm not moping. Things aren't good." I told him what happened at Cowboy School. "What if Ringo is a better horse for Conrad?"

"Don't get down on yourself. Ringo and those Mason paints are just looking for an excuse to squeeze you out. You've got the good life, and Ringo's a remuda horse. He wants what you have. He doesn't play fair. Watch your back with that one."

"Okay, I get that Ringo is jealous and wants to oust me, but why are the paints helping him? What's in it for them?"

I sidled closer to Roany. We had out differences, but down deep I knew he liked me.

"They're running scared. Levi and Randy are fickle. If Cody or Conrad wins, then the Mason boys will blame their horses and send Trip and Trap off to the remuda."

That sent my head reeling. "Wow, does that mean Ringo intends to throw the competition so one of the Mason boys can win?"

"That would be my guess, yes."

Fear joined the sadness that had been weighing me down. "But, how can I fight back? I'm injured. Ringo's got me hemmed in."

Roany snorted. "You might be a lot of things, Gunpowder, but I never took you for a quitter."

I tossed my head and winced against the pain that shot through my shoulder. "I'm not a quitter. What can I do to get healed faster? The competition is in two weeks."

"Glad you asked. I've been thinking about it, and it's called physical therapy."

That sounded hard and painful, but I wasn't afraid to do what it took to achieve my goals.

"We'll train at night," Roany said.

What? My hopes sprung. "We? You'll help?"

"Gunpowder, what's the one thing you've got that Ringo doesn't have?"

"Umm…a thicker mane?"

Roany burst out laughing. "No, you silly cowpony. You've got real *friends*."

$\mho$ $\mho$ $\mho$

The next two weeks were some of the toughest I've ever experienced. Every evening after school, Roany and I would practice together. He started out by trotting me up and down the shed row of the stables. Then we jumped bales of hay and finally, toward the end, ran at a full lope up and down the pasture.

"Let's go, let's go." Roany pushed me as hard as if he were a football coach. "Faster, faster."

During the day, I'd workout in the corral at Cowboy School with Chief and Scarbutt urging me on as I cantered around in circles.

The day before the competition, on the way home from school, I trotted alongside Conrad and Ringo on the lead rope the entire way.

My shoulder was healing.

"You're doing so well, Gunpowder, it won't be long before I'll be riding you again," Conrad said.

My pulse beat faster, and my hopes soared. Even if I didn't get to ride in the competition, I'd soon take back my rightful place as Conrad's working horse.

Beside me, Ringo backed his ears, curled his upper lip, and swished his tail.

When we got to the ranch barn, I noticed Mr. Winks had the cow trailer hooked up to the pickup. Roany, Maggie, and Tuffy were loaded up in the pickup and ready to go.

Maggie was smiling and Tuffy was wagging his tail so fast

I thought he would take off like a helicopter.

"Headed somewhere, Mr. Winks?" asked Conrad.

"*We're* headed somewhere. I've been waiting for you to get home."

"That's what I was hoping you would say." Gleefully, Conrad tossed his hat in the air. "Let me put Gunpowder in the corral, and I'll load Ringo."

"I thought maybe this time you could give Ringo a rest and saddle up Gunpowder." Mr. Winks had a twinkle in his eye. "I saw Doc Riley at the post office this morning, and he said that some light work would do Gunpowder a world of good."

"Really?" Conrad beamed.

Really? I thought, my heart leaping with joy.

"We only have a handful of cow-calf pairs to work, and I bet we can get them done before dark."

Have you ever seen a horse have a temper tantrum? Let me tell you, it ain't very pretty. Ringo swished his tail, stomped his front hooves, and whinnied like a spoiled colt being weaned from his mama.

Conrad unsaddled Ringo, and gave him a quick brushing, and left him in his stall. Ha!

Then he put a fresh saddle blanket and saddle on my back, and cinched it up tight.

It was the best feeling in the world. I didn't realize how much I had missed the saddle.

Conrad loaded me next to Roany, and I glanced over my shoulder at Ringo.

He gave me a stare so cold it that would freeze Johnson

grass in the summer.

I wanted to stick out my tongue at him, but decided to be a good sport. Enjoying the sun on my face, I turned to Roany who was standing beside me in the trailer. "Just like old times, huh?"

"If you say so, Gunpowder."

"I do!" I crowed, happier than I'd been since that mama cow plodded into me.

"I guess I have been missing your annoying presence." Roany sighed as if I was a royal pain in his side.

I grinned.

Yep, just like old times.

CHAPTER SEVEN

CHEAP SHOT

The county caliche roads were bumpy and dusty. I'll have to admit, the bumps were rough on my shoulder, but I wasn't about to tell a soul. Not even Roany.

We unloaded and started sifting through the mesquite trees, looking for any new born calves that needed vaccinating.

A calf jumped out in front of us and scurried off.

I startled, gasped.

"Whoa, Gunpowder! You almost jumped out from under me!" Conrad hollered.

Mr. Winks rode up. "It may take a while before Gunpowder gets over being nervous in the pasture. You don't forget a thing like being mauled by a mean tiger-striped cow."

Conrad patted my neck. "It's okay, buddy, that old cow and her calf have probably jumped a dozen fences by now and are grazing somewhere in the next county."

I sure hoped he was right. I didn't ever want to see that mean mama cow again.

After that, I went on full alert. I heard every leaf that rustled and every blade of grass that swayed from the wind.

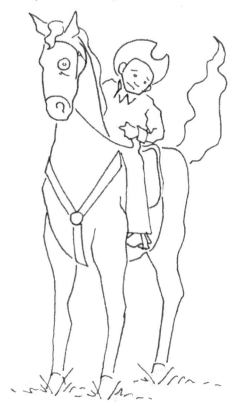

"Brrr," a baby calf bellowed from the tree line.

I wheeled around, pulse pounding to see a beautiful, peaceful, slow-moving mama Angus cow and her calf. Their black shiny coats glistened in the sun as they waddled from the tall grass where they had bedded down for an afternoon nap.

Whew. I slowly let out a sigh of relief.

"Well, lookie there." Conrad swirled his lasso, making a loop. "This one's gonna be easy as catching fish in a barrel. Let's go, boy."

I wanted to go toward the cow and calf, but my legs locked up. It took every ounce of effort that I had to put one hoof in front of the other.

"Gunpowder, what's wrong?" Conrad lightly prodded me with his spurs, not wanting to push me too hard.

I took a few steps toward the calf. I had to get over my fear of being attacked again. I had to swallow my fear and get my boy back on my saddle permanently.

The calf put his nose up and sniffed. His mama came up behind him and pushed him toward Conrad with her nose as if she knew we were there to help.

I nudged the calf into rope-catching range. Conrad delivered his loop slick around the calf's neck and stepped off my back. He vaccinated the calf, turned him loose, and we headed on our way.

Okay, not so hard. But my pulse was still hammering. I took a few deep breaths to calm down. I couldn't let one scary incident ruin me. I had to stay strong.

By the time we arrived back at the barn, Ringo had cooled off from his temper tantrum and was eating the hay in the bin.

Conrad led me to the hitching post, unsaddled me, and brushed me out. Gently, he rubbed my scar. "Okay, buddy, you're getting extra oats tonight for doing so well."

Ringo stopped eating and gave me the evil eye again.

The sun went down, and the moon came up and lit the

night sky. Conrad walked down the trail headed home. Mr. Winks had let Maggie and Tuffy into the house to sleep on the wood floor next to the stove because the nights were cooling off.

All was quiet in the barn.

The cool night air caused my shoulder to ache. I dozed off and on, thrashing around, and trying to get comfortable. Finally, I drifted off to sleep.

Out of nowhere, that tiger-striped cow charged from the brush, her horns were sharp like cavalry swords, and her eyes were bright red and…

"Wake up, Gunpowder! Wake up!"

My eyes flew open, and I saw Roany standing over me, bumping me with his nose. "You're having another nightmare about that tiger-striped cow."

I got up and limped around for a minute. "How did you know I was dreaming about that cow?"

"You were hollering in your sleep."

I must have slept wrong because my shoulder was hurting almost as much as it had been the day after the cow horned me. I winced.

"You better stay quiet and quit limping unless you want Ringo to see you," Roany warned. "He'll find a way to use it against you."

"What can I do to quit having those dreams and being scared every time Conrad and I ride through the pasture?"

"Only one solution."

"What's that?" I swung my ears forward to pick up his wisdom.

"You're gonna have to confront your fears."

That wasn't what I wanted to hear. "How do I do that?"

"Meet up with that cow again and show her who's boss."

"But how do I find her?"

"I don't know where she is, but that's what you'll have to do if you want to end the nightmares and stop being afraid."

My bottom lip trembled. Much as I hated hearing this, Roany was right. I had to get tough and face that cow again.

"You know what I do when I get scared?" he asked.

"I didn't know that rough, tough Roany ever got scared." I grinned thankful that he was helping me.

"Once," he said. "I got scared *once* when I was a little colt."

"Haha, what did you do to overcome your fears when you were a colt?"

Roany picked his head up and poked his chest out. "I looked that fear straight in the eye and didn't back down."

"Yeah? I'd like to see you do that when a crazy, mean, tiger-striped cow is running straight toward you with red eyes burning, and her Texas-size horns are going for your shoulder."

"I see your point," he said. "It's normal to be scared, but you can't let fear stop you from living your life."

"Roany, I've been thinking. I've been running the incident over and over, and I'm not sure that I would have done anything differently."

"You did everything you could."

"It's just not fair. I would give my life for Conrad, and I almost did."

"We all know that."

"Now, I'm half-crippled and sore, and as much as I want to be completely healed, I'm not."

"It's only been a few weeks, Gunpowder. Give it time." He was trying to comfort me, but I was on a roll and feeling a little sorry for myself.

"To top it off," I went on. "I've got this hot shot Ringo trying to steal my boy away, and I can't do anything about it. I'm useless!"

Roany squinted his steely eyes and gave me a look that would make an oak tree wilt. "You're whining, Gunpowder, and if there's one thing I can't stand, it's a whiner. Get over yourself. Stop with the pity party!"

I snuffled. "Okay, you're right. I'll try, Roany, I'll try."

Roany twitched his ears. "Gunpowder, have you ever seen a cow act that wild before?"

I thought a minute. "No, I can't say that I have, and Conrad and I have been around a lot of cattle."

"Would you say the tiger-striped cow was in her right mind?"

"Nope."

"Do you think she just might have been as scared of you as you were her and all she cared about was protecting her baby the way you were protecting Conrad?"

I rolled that over in my mind. "Maybe."

"If you can figure out why she acted the way she did, maybe your fear will go away."

He made a good point, and as I drifted off back to sleep, I planned how I was going to find that cow and face her again.

In the morning, I got up early to stretch my shoulder and

walk around the corral, my mind still on what had happened the evening before.

"What's wrong, Gunpowder, your shoulder hurting?" Ringo asked in a snarky tone.

"Nothing you need to be concerned about. Just a little tight is all."

"Yeah, I bet."

"I imagine you're worried since Conrad took me out to work calves yesterday."

Ringo snorted. "Worried? About you?"

"Yep, that's it. You're worried that your golden days are coming to an end, and that you'll have to go back to the remuda."

He backed his ears and narrowed his flinty eyes. "Gunpowder, you better be careful what you say."

Before I could come up with a quick retort, Conrad showed up, and we took off for Cowboy School. He rode Ringo, and I trotted alongside of them just like we'd been doing for the last two weeks.

It was a beautiful, crisp morning in the Texas Hill Country. Mesquites had lost their leaves and the dove and quail were moving slower from the damp coolness. If I hadn't been so worried about what Ringo had up his sleeve, I would have slowed down to take in the beauty.

Ringo was ripe for trouble. He picked up the pace, moving into a trot.

I struggled to keep up with him.

"Whoa," Conrad pulled back on the reins, but Ringo chomped down on the bridle bit and just kept trotting, acting like an immature colt.

It crossed my mind to come to a full stop and plunk right down in the dirt. But that would have most likely jerked Conrad off the saddle since he was holding onto the lead rope.

Grunting, I started trotting faster than Ringo.

He couldn't stand that and quickened his stride.

I broke out into a lope, and just before it turned into a full on horse race, an old timer pulled out onto the county road in his broken-down ranch truck, bringing us to an abrupt halt.

Both Ringo and I shook our heads, irritated with the truck. I backed my ears and showed my teeth, and he did the same to me.

"Guys, y'all stop that!" Conrad scolded.

After we got to Cowboy School and were put in the corrals, Ringo immediately sidled over to the Trip and Trap.

"They're up to something," I said, and told Chief, Scarbutt, and Oso what had happened between me and Ringo.

Chief nodded. "Yes, sir, they are."

"None of trust that outlaw Ringo," Oso added.

"You're not alone, Gunpowder," Scarbutt said. "We've always got your back."

That afternoon while Mr. Barton, the kids and their horses went to gather steers for sorting practice. I did a lot of stretching and walking around my corral. An hour later, the kids and their horses drove the cattle from the school ranch into the arena. Ringo and Conrad in the lead.

Levi stood up in the stirrups, and asked his brother, "Did you see how Ringo stopped that white-faced steer from breaking from the herd?"

"I've never seen a cowpony move so quick," Randy said. "Conrad, that horse is way too good for you."

"Yeah." Levi snickered. "He needs a *good* rider like Randy or me."

"Hush up, Levi!" Mr. Barton scolded. "Get those steers in the arena, so we'll have time to practice before you go home."

Levi looked sullen but shut his mouth.

Mr. Barton clapped his hands, commanding everyone's attention. "Listen up class." He waited for the kids to grow quiet before continuing, "When you hear your name called, ride into the arena."

I rested my chin on the top board of the corral fence to watch what was going on at the arena from across the expanse of schoolyard.

Mr. Barton sank his hands on his hips. "I'll call out a number for you to start with, then you sort the cattle in numerical order, just like we discussed before. Y'all remember that?"

All the kids bobbed their heads in unison. Ringo slid me a sidelong glance, and I wished like anything that I was over there with Conrad instead of that outlaw.

"I'll blow the whistle when a minute is up. Remember, if your horse bites or kicks at a steer, you are disqualified. Remember, this is just practice, so you'll be ready for the competition. Any questions?"

None of the kids raised their hands.

"Good. Ashley, you and Scarbutt are up first. You'll start with steer number three."

Ashley and her horse went right to work. Number three steer sorted easily, then four, five, six, and seven before the whistle blew.

"Good job!" Conrad clapped.

"That Scarbutt can really sort 'em out quick," Juan said.

The Mason boys went next, and each sorted three steers. Then it was Cody and Chief. They had some difficulty with the red-faced steer and only sorted two. Oso did well for being such a big horse. He and Juan sorted three steers.

"And finally," Mr. Barton announced. "Conrad and Ringo."

I watched closely, determined not to miss a move.

"Number four!" shouted Mr. Barton.

Ringo and Conrad had no problem with number four. The number five steer jumped from side to side but Ringo stayed right with him every step. He moved so fast, Conrad had trouble staying up with him and his foot almost slipped from the stirrup.

Number six went without much resistance, then seven and eight…

The kids started cheering because he had enough time for one more, but number nine was the red-faced steer that had given Chief and Cody so much trouble.

That red-face steer ran into the corner and refused to move.

Ringo signaled Trip and Trap with a swish of his tail, and they started neighing and making all kinds of racket.

What were those two up to?

Mr. Barton and the kids looked their way, but I didn't. I kept my eye on my buddy riding that outlaw horse. I didn't trust Ringo any farther than I could kick him.

When everyone was focused on the paints, and no one

was watching him, not even Conrad, Ringo reached down and bit that red-faced steer on the hip.

The steer jumped and bolted for the gate.

Mr. Barton spun back around and blew the whistle. "Six steers for Conrad and Ringo! Top score."

All the kids cheered and applauded.

But, I was fuming. Ringo had cheated. He'd gotten Trip and Trap to help him cheat. He was out for glory, and he didn't care what he had to do to win.

Not knowing what his horse had done, Conrad grinned from ear to ear. He patted Ringo on the neck and told him what a great cowpony he was.

I seethed. Yeah, a great outlaw. Cheating was what Ringo

was great at.

"Great job, Conrad," Juan congratulated him.

Full of sour grapes, Randy Mason said, "You better hang on a little tighter next time, Conrad. That Ringo is one fast cowpony at sorting."

"Yeah," said Levi. "Faster than you can handle."

Conrad led the prancing, proud Ringo through the stables and tied him to the hitching post, so all the kids could come over to rub and pat him.

Ringo might be amazing at sorting cattle, but he was a cheater, and the paints were helping him.

That was more than I could chew. I had to turn away.

Mr. Barton blew his whistle to get everyone's attention. "We're celebrating sorting practice with a Coke float. Tie your horses up, and let's raid the freezer."

Once the kids and Mr. Barton left the stables, I strolled over Ringo who was talking and laughing with the paints.

"I guess you three think you're pretty smart getting away with biting that steer," I said.

"I don't know what you're talking about." Ringo gave me a blank stare, but underneath I could tell he was taunting me.

"You may have gotten away with cheating today, but I'll make sure you won't get away with it again."

Ringo grinned and said, "You're just jealous because you're crippled, and all washed up."

Trip laughed. "That's right, Gunpowder, you're all washed up and no good anymore. You might as well go back to Bangs and be a town horse again for some little kid."

"You don't belong at Cowboy School anymore," Trap said. "And, you don't belong at the Mesquite Bean."

I stuck my chin in the air. "Think what you will, but I've been getting better every day and I'll be ready for the competition. Conrad will see I'm healed, and he'll choose me instead of Ringo."

Ringo's face turned a mean shade of red. He backed both ears, gritted his teeth, and said in the meanest voice I ever heard, "You say one more word, Gunpowder, and you're gonna get it."

I backed my ears too, squared my shoulders and gave him a determined stare. "Don't threaten me, Ringo."

One of the paints kicked the metal barn.

I turned to see what was happening.

A sudden jolt hit my bad shoulder, jarring all way down to my tail. Red jets of burning pain blurred my vision. It felt like a lightning bolt had struck me. My knees went weak and my stomach turned sick. I glanced around searching for the source of my suffering.

Ringo stood there laughing. He'd used the same ploy on me that he'd used to cheat in the sorting. Trip and Trap distracted my attention while Ringo landed a cheap shot, slamming a double-barreled kick into my shoulder with both of his back legs.

I could see the imprint of his horseshoes embedded into my healing hide.

My shoulder throbbed with piercing pain, my head spun, and I went to the ground. I gritted my teeth and tried to stand, but just couldn't bear my weight. The last thing I wanted was to be down when Ringo and the paints were peering over me with smirks and evil eyes.

"I told you to watch what you say, Gunpowder." Ringo seethed between clenched teeth.

"Looks like you don't have a leg to stand on." Trip laughed.

"Gunpowder!" Conrad shouted and came running toward me, his friends following after him. "Are you okay?"

I tried to get up again, but it still hurt too much to stand.

Conrad sank to his knees beside me. He smelled like cola and vanilla ice cream. I hated that I'd spoiled it for him, enjoying his Coke float, but I sure was glad he was here. "What happened, boy? Are you okay?"

I hurt so badly I couldn't even nod.

"I'll go tell Mr. Barton." Ashley ran back to the schoolhouse. A minute later, she returned with him.

"Step aside, Conrad," Mr. Barton said. "And let me have a look."

Conrad scooted over and Mr. Barton crouched beside me. He gently fingered my shoulder.

I flinched and tried not to cry out.

"Looks like he took a pretty bad hit on his shoulder." Mr. Barton shook his head. "The wound is bleeding at the suture line."

"Oh no." Conrad worried his bottom lip with his top teeth.

Mr. Barton shook his head ruefully. "This is such a shame. Gunpowder was doing so well."

Yeah, until the cheater Ringo kicked me.

"Conrad, jump on Ringo and get to the Mesquite Bean. Tell Mr. Winks to bring his trailer. We need to get Gunpowder to Doc Riley."

"Yes, sir!" Conrad sprung onto Ringo's back, and they took off.

I couldn't help wondering if Ringo would find some way to delay getting me to Doc Riley. I wouldn't put it past him.

Mr. Barton turned back to me. "Cody, why don't you grab a halter and lead rope, and let's see if we can get Gunpowder to his feet."

Cody put the halter and lead rope on me. Juan and Ashley stood to my left, Mr. Barton on my right.

"Okay, Gunpowder, come on up, buddy," Cody urged tugging on the rope.

I put my three good legs under myself and pushed hard. The pain was still really bad, shooting in all directions. I was wobbly and staggered a bit, but managed to stay on my feet.

Before long, we heard Mr. Winks' truck and trailer bouncing down the county road. Conrad on Ringo followed right behind at a full run.

The rig pulled to a sliding stop in front of the schoolhouse.

"Back your trailer on up to the stables, Mr. Winks," Mr. Barton called.

Mr. Winks gave thumbs up, turned his rig around and backed up to the stable gate. He got out, lifting his cowboy hat and scratching his head. "What the heck happened?"

Mr. Barton shot a suspicious look over at the Mason boys and their paints. "We are really not sure, but I have an idea. I'll have to tell you later though. All ears don't need to hear."

"Gotcha," said Mr. Winks.

CHAPTER EIGHT

COWBOY UP

When we pulled up to the vet clinic, Doc Riley was walking out to his pickup, headed home for the evening.

"Sorry, but we got one more for ya, Doc," Mr. Winks said.

"Oh, that's okay, that's the name of the game in the vet business, always on call. What can I do for you?" Doc Riley put his keys back in his pocket.

"You'll see a familiar face in the trailer," said Mr. Barton.

Grunting, Doc Riley moseyed to the back of the trailer, and peered in through the paneled slates at me. "What's wrong, my friend?"

Doc Riley had become my friend, and I was glad to see him this time. Maybe he could take this fresh pain away.

"Let's get you out, and take a look-see." Doc Riley opened the back gate of the trailer.

Unloading was a lot worse than loading because when I

Doc Riley gave me a shot to help with the pain, wrapped an ice bag around my shoulder, and led me to the same stall I stayed in before.

Conrad, Mr. Barton, and Mr. Winks drove off with Ringo in the trailer. He stomped the floor and popped his tail, laughing the whole time.

If I hadn't been in so much pain, I would have been mad as a hornet.

After Doc Riley turned out the lights and left the clinic, I limped over to the hay left in the stall and munched on it.

"You must really want attention bad to fake another injury," said the voice of one smart aleck goat.

"Hey, Strawberry," I replied, "When did they let you out of goat jail?"

"Haha, you're a funny one, Gunpowder. What happened this time to the mightiest cowpony in the West?"

I told him how Ringo and the paints were putting the squeeze on me to get me out of the picture, so Ringo could move into being the permanent team of Conrad and Ringo.

Strawberry shook his head. "Drama, drama, drama! You horses are always competing."

"Goats aren't competitive?"

"Nah, goats are usually just looking for some good gossip and something to chew on."

"I wish that's all Ringo was looking for," I muttered.

"Well, I just dropped by to check on you. See you in the morning. I'm on my way to chew on that lead rope that Doc Riley left hanging from the hook."

"Have fun," I said.

? soreness kept me from sleeping well. In the middle
night, I was awakened by Buck trashing around in the
He was mumbling in his sleep, crying out about the
ow."

y, Buck, wake up! You're dreaming about that tiger-
cow."

h?" He sounded groggy.

ke up." I peered over the stall at him. He was lying
vet with sweat and trembling all over. I sure felt sorry
. I knew what that was like. "You gotta get her out of
ad, horse."

ly, he got to his feet. "Yeah, you're right."

you want to talk about that happened? Maybe it will

. yawned. "Maybe."

you don't have to talk if you don't want to," I
aled, suddenly worried that if he talked about the
have nightmares too, if I ever got to sleep.

n't mind talking," Buck said. "I was grazing on some
grass minding my own business, when she came out
ere and rammed me in the side with her head."

ced. Been there, had the scar to prove it.

impact knocked me down, and when I tried to get
harged and hit me again."

a mean one," I said.

y time I'd get up, she'd charge me again and hook me
horns."

t must have been scary."

bet," Buck said. "She just wouldn't quit. I kicked her

with everything I had, but it didn't seem to faze her."

"How did you get away from her?"

"She finally stopped coming at me when her calf startle and ran off. She turned and followed after it."

"I've been there, my friend. I completely understand, bu you'll heal, and you will be good as new," I said, trying to re his worries, but my own worries were taking over.

It wasn't fair what had happened to me, but how cou I allow this mean, tiger-striped cow to ruin my life? No, mean, how could the outlaw Ringo be allowed to ruin m life? He was the one who reopened my healing wound. I fe so helpless.

Buck would heal and go on living life as being Doc Riley cowpony, living at the clinic and ranch. But what about m Would I ever be a good cowpony again?

Maybe Doc Riley would be interested in another injure horse just to have for light riding. Maybe he had a grandchil that needed a babysitter. Maybe it was time for me to be pu out to pasture.

A lump clogged my throat. I wasn't ready to give up m life with Conrad.

"Gunpowder, your eyes are swimming with worry. What stirring around between those ears of yours?" Buck asked.

I lowered my head, glanced down. "What that tiger-stripe cow did to us has made me realize I'm probably finished bein Conrad's cowpony. I must accept that I will never be as goo as I was before, and that puts Ringo as Conrad's number on cowpony. It's just not fair."

Buck raised an eyebrow and cocked his head. "Yep, you'r

I couldn't believe Conrad was so mesmerized with Ringo.

I pushed those woe-is-me thoughts out of my head and remembered what Buck had said. It was time for me to cowpony up.

Using the trick Buck had taught me while I was at Doc Riley's, I eased up to the gate. With my top lip, I flipped up the handle on the latch. The first time through, I didn't move fast enough and the latch fell back down before I could unlatch it.

Undaunted, I tried again. This time, I flipped the handle up with my top lip and managed to quickly catch it with my bottom lip and kept it from locking. With the handle caught between my teeth, I slid the lever, while at the same time pushing against the gate with my chest.

Ta-da!

The gate swung open, and I was free.

I glanced over one shoulder and then the other to make sure no one was watching. No point in making a great escape if I got caught.

It's funny how people respond whenever they see a horse outside a fence without someone leading or riding them. They always yell, "Loose Horse!" and then run after you as if they are the horse police.

I limped down the gravel driveway headed for Cowboy School. On the way past Conrad's house, I saw Seven, my old friend, grazing in her corral near the road. She raised her head and mooed a soft greeting. My heart lifted at the sight of her familiar face.

Making sure no humans were around, I eased up to the fence and rested my chin on top of the railing.

"You gonna stand there gawking all day, or are you going to tell me how you got out of your enclosure at the Mesquite Bean?" she asked in her nasally twang.

"Just admiring your corral. Kind of makes me homesick. I dropped by to see a friendly face."

"What's got you down, my friend?"

"My healing is going slowly." For some reason, I didn't tell her about going to Cowboy School and the trouble with Ringo.

"I'm sorry that old tiger-striped cow got hold of you, Gunpowder." Seven's eyes were sympathetic. "She's a wild one and loves to make life tough on cowhands and their horses."

"Where did you hear about her?" I asked.

"Even though I spend most of my time close to the house, Herman and Anne will stake me out close to the pasture fence for good grass. Sometimes, the cows and their calves will stop by to chat, and you know how all the mama cows can be. They love to gossip. Keeps me informed."

I nodded. "I see."

"Why do you ask?"

"I wonder why this cow who haunts my dreams, likes to make life so hard on horses. She got both me and Doc Riley's horse, Buck. Is it just fear? Do you think she's afraid we're going to hurt her baby?"

Seven glanced around to make sure no one was listening. "Rumor has it that she had a bad experience with a horse in her calf-hood, and that's why she hates horses."

"What kind of bad experience?"

"No one knows for sure." Seven flicked a fly from her back

with a swish of her tail. "Maybe, a cowboy and cowpony had been too rough with her when she was a calf.

"Or, perhaps some outlaw horse had kicked her or bit at her when running through the herd," I mused, thinking of Ringo.

"There is no way to know for sure without talking to her, and that's probably not going to happen. She doesn't stay in one pasture very long, and I hear she and her calf can jump a fence, no problem."

"Seven, you've given me something to think about. I better get back to my corral before Mr. Winks and Roany get back. They'll be worried if I'm not around. See ya, old friend, and thanks!" I trotted off.

She gave a long mooo and bobbed her head goodbye.

It's kind of funny how your brain starts to think differently about someone that you don't like when you learned more about them. That tiger-striped cow had haunted my thoughts and dreams, and now I was starting to maybe feel sorry for her. If Seven was right about her calf-hood, maybe she was just scared and trying to protect her calf.

CHAPTER NINE

CHAMPION SORTER

The day of the competition finally arrived. The day I'd been dreading because Conrad would be riding Ringo and not me.

Conrad showed up to the barn earlier than usual. He had on his best bright blue western shirt, blue jeans, gray felt hat, and cowboy boots polished to a high shine.

He gave Ringo an extra good brushing and combing.

Mr. Winks strolled into the barn. "Good luck, Conrad."

"Thanks, but if Ringo does his magic today, like he did in practice, I won't need luck," Conrad said.

"Don't get overly confident. Luck always has a hand in it," Mr. Winks said. "No matter how skilled you and your horse are. Just do your best."

"Yes, sir." Conrad ducked his head.

Herman and Anne's pickup bounced up the ranch drive,

horn honking. Herman parked outside the barn and stuck his head out the open window. "Are you ready, son?"

"Yes, sir, I've got Ringo brushed, and I'm shined up." Conrad chuckled.

"How about we take Gunpowder along?" Anne suggested. "I can't stand the thought of him missing out on your big day."

"Good idea," Mr. Winks said. "I should have thought of that myself.

They were going to take me? Yippee! I wanted to hop up, but I was too achy. Slowly, I stood and stretched my shoulder.

Herman slipped a halter over my ears.

Anne gently examined my shoulder. "Poor fella."

"Let's put Gunpowder in the front of the trailer," Mr. Winks said. "Then Roany. We'll load Ringo last since he's the biggest."

Thank heavens I wasn't going in the trailer behind Ringo. I didn't trust that ornery outlaw not to kick me.

U U U

At the Cowboy School arena, Scarbutt and Chief were tied to the top rail of the fence. Ashley and Cody pitched horseshoes with the other kids, while they waited for the sorting competition to begin.

As we unloaded, Scarbutt nickered and Chief whinnied to welcome me. But when Ringo came out of the trailer saddled up and ready to go, I could see the pity in their eyes.

"You come on over and be with us today." Anne led me to their pickup.

Herman opened the tailgate of the pickup. Anne pulled out a big red carton of homemade cookies and a big jug of iced tea, for anyone that may need a snack. My favorite were the oatmeal cookies. She fed me one.

Yum. That pepped me up for a couple of minutes. But, my heart sank lower and lower as I watched the kids loping their horses in the arena for warm up.

There was Conrad in his shiny competition cowboy clothes, laughing, and riding Ringo in front of the crowd as they packed into the bleachers. It made my stomach tie up in knots so bad that I didn't even want another oatmeal cookie.

Mr. Barton stepped up to the microphone. "Competitors, please exit the arena, and we will get the sorting started."

The kids on their horses passed by. Scarbutt, Chief, and Oso gave a howdy nicker to me. That boosted my spirits until

Ringo and the Mason paints came prancing by, swishing their tails, and laughing.

"Please stand for the National Anthem and a prayer for the safety of all the competitors and their cowponies," Mr. Barton announced.

Ashley Weatherford's parents, Scott and Becky, did a beautiful job playing the guitar and singing the National Anthem. Then Mr. Barton said a prayer, and we were ready to begin.

"Ladies and Gentlemen, I want to welcome you to the first annual Cowboy School sorting competition. These boys and girls have been practicing their ranching skills at Cowboy School every afternoon."

The spectators applauded and cheered.

Over the microphone, Mr. Barton explained the rules. "As soon as the single rider and his or her horse cross over the white painted line and move toward the cattle, time begins. The team has one minute to sort out as many cattle as possible in numerical order according to the numbers painted on their back. If a steer gets by out of order, the rider and horse will not receive a score at all. If the horse bites, kicks, or paws at a steer, that competitor will be disqualified. Mr. Winks and his horse Roany of the Mesquite Bean Ranch will run block at the gate for every competitor. We have a panel of three judges to keep time and count the steers."

The panel of judges, all experienced cowboys, waved at the crowd from where they sat at the front of the arena.

The kids drew for the order. Cody and Chief went first, followed by Randy Mason and his paint, Ashley and Scarbutt,

Levi Mason and his paint, Juan and Oso, and finally Conrad and Ringo in the final spot.

"Let's get the show started," Mr. Barton said.

As usual Cody and Chief put in a strong, competitive showing. Sorting five steers out of the herd in their minute. The Mason boys and their paints let some steers go by out of order and received a no score, and I hate to say it, but it served them right for helping Ringo cheat at practice.

Ashley and Scarbutt dug in and really hustled. They sorted six steers in their minute. All three judges gave them a score of six out of ten. The top score so far.

Juan and his big brown horse Oso only sorted four. They had trouble with one steer that was hardheaded and just didn't want to go out, which costs them about twenty seconds.

"Ladies and Gentlemen, our final team is Conrad and Ringo. This horse and rider teamed up after Conrad's main horse, Gunpowder, was injured by a wild cow in a ranching accident. Gunpowder has joined us today and is standing on the sidelines supporting his team. Let's give a big hand to Gunpowder the Cowpony, and hope he gets well soon."

The crowd applauded.

Feeling proud and honored, I popped my tail and raised my head above the top rail of the arena and give a big whinny.

"Okay, Conrad and Ringo, it's your turn," Mr. Barton said. "You'll start with steer number three."

Without hesitating, Conrad rode Ringo across the line, and the time started.

I held my breath. I wanted Conrad to win, but I did not want Ringo to best me.

Ringo approached the herd, rolled his nostrils, backed his ears, and rode directly at number three.

Fear set in the herd immediately from being bitten and pawed so much at practice by Ringo. Number three went out, almost without any effort by Conrad and Ringo.

Quickly followed by four, five, six. Number seven was a little hesitant, but eight bumped him forward, and nine followed out right behind. The buzzer went off. Time was up.

The crowd cheered wildly.

Conrad pulled the reins up. Ringo pranced around. Then Conrad doffed his hat and waved to the crowd.

The panel of judges held up their score cards. Seven out of ten!

Mr. Barton's voice cracked with excitement. "That was an amazing run with seven steers culled from the herd. Conrad and Ringo are the champion sorters!"

Conrad and Ashley were awarded a cash prize and new halters for first and second places. They shook hands with all the other competitors, even Randy and Levi Mason.

"Mom, Dad, Mr. Winks," Conrad hollered, riding up to

his parents' pickup. "We did it. Ringo is an amazing horse. We won thirty dollars' cash and this new halter!"

"Well, congratulations, Conrad!" said Mr. Winks.

I took a big gulp that hurt all the way down.

"Gotta go, ya'll, Mr. Barton wants us all to gather for a picture for the Brownwood newspaper." As Conrad rode off, Ringo cut me with a steely smirk.

$$\mathcal{U} \quad \mathcal{U} \quad \mathcal{U}$$

The next evening was a big celebration at the Mesquite Bean Ranch.

Anne brought her famous apple, cherry, and pecan pies. Herman cooked a big brisket over the fire pit. Mr. Winks churned homemade vanilla ice cream. The kids and their horses played tag in the front pasture.

The game is just like regular tag but on horses. Everyone was having fun except me and Roany. We were stuck watching from the corral.

"Did you hear about the big cow hunt this weekend?" he asked.

"What are you talking about?" I asked.

Roany is the kind of horse that doesn't say much, but when he does, it means something and you better listen.

"I overheard Mr. Winks talking to a bunch of ranchers about it."

"What were they saying?"

"Well, hold your horseshoes on, and I'll tell you. That tiger-striped cow and her calf that got you and Buck, also ran one of Mr. Mason's mares into a fence and horned her too."

"My goodness, she's a bad one!" I said.

"Yes, sir, she is. She was spotted just north of Mesquite Bean Ranch and they think she's grazing the green grass in Box Canyon."

"It is delicious grass," I mused.

"They're looking to start a posse of experienced ranch horses to go after her."

"You think she will give up?" I asked.

"Not a chance, Gunpowder, not a chance."

"I sure wish that I could go," I said feeling washed up and useless.

CHAPTER
TEN

NEVER QUIT

Early Sunday morning, just before dawn, Mr. Winks came into the barn where he brushed and saddled Roany.

Mr. Mason and three of his ranch cowboys pulled up in their big truck and trailer. Right after them, Doc Riley and Mr. Barton pulled up in Doc's veterinarian pickup. They were pulling a small trailer, hauling Doc's second-string ranch horse since Buck was still recuperating, and Mr. Barton's big brown ranch horse.

"Good morning, men," Mr. Winks greeted them. "I asked y'all to come early because Conrad is still in bed. This isn't a hunt for kids. Plus, I figured we could get this job over and still have time for church."

The men agreed.

"Grab some coffee and biscuits from the fire pit, then we'll head out."

The men swallowed a quick cup of strong cowboy coffee and stuffed biscuits in their vest pockets. They mounted up and headed for the north pasture.

They weren't gone ten minutes, and who do you think came bouncing up the hill to feed Ringo and Old News Gunpowder some morning oats? Yep, it was Conrad.

"Hey, Ringo, why are all these pickups and trailers here?" Conrad asked.

Ringo looked off into the distance.

"Where is Mr. Winks and Roany?" Conrad took off his cowboy hat and scratched the top of his head. "Why didn't they take us with them?"

Ringo just buried his head in his bucket of oats and pretended to not understand. He definitely didn't want to go after the tiger-striped cow. He probably thought he should only be a competition horse in the arena since the big win. Or, maybe he was too scared.

Conrad walked over to the gate where the tall grass and weeds had been mashed down. "We gotta catch up to everyone. I wonder why they didn't ask me to go. I guess, maybe, they thought I would want to sleep in after the big night of fun. Well, they're wrong. Let's go, Ringo."

Conrad came into the corral,

Ringo turned around, putting his rear-end to Conrad. "What's wrong, Ringo? Don't you want to go?"

I just wanted to laugh and say, "Conrad, your *awesome* Ringo is too much of a coward!"

Conrad got the bridle and came after Ringo.

Ringo ran from one corner of the corral to the other,

trying to duck away.

But, Conrad was determined. He cornered Ringo. "What's the matter, is it too early?"

Ringo snorted.

Conrad started saddling him.

If Conrad went hunting for that tiger-striped cow on cowardly Ringo, he could be in real danger.

I flipped the handle of the corral gate trying to get Conrad's attention. Maybe he would take me instead of Ringo. I trotted around the corral, splashed water in my trough, and whinnied as loud as I could.

Nothing seemed to work. Conrad just gave me a disgusted look and scolded, "Calm down, Gunpowder!"

Conrad finally got Ringo saddled after a lot of fidgeting and side-stepping. He put a boot in the stirrup and swung into the saddle.

Immediately Ringo pranced away from the north pasture gate.

"Whoa, Ringo!" Conrad pulled him around and went through the gate. "Let's catch up to them. Yhaa!" yelled Conrad.

Here I was, left alone in the barn, just me, myself, and I. There was no way that I was going to sit by and let anything happen to Conrad. I'd gotten so good at letting myself out, I didn't even have to rehearse the steps that Buck told me. All I had to do was get through the gate and follow the trail.

By the looks of the tracks, Conrad was having a hard time keeping Ringo going straight and headed to Box Canyon. Let's just see what kind of great cowpony Ringo is outside an arena, where he can't cheat and let him try to scare that tiger-striped, big horn, horse eating cow!

The north pasture was rough country. It had lots of cactus, mesquite trees, and rocky ground to cover which slowed me down some. My shoulder ached, but each time I thought of the tiger-striped cow being in the same pasture with Conrad and Ringo, I picked up my pace. A little pain wasn't going to keep me from being there for Conrad.

In the distance I heard Mr. Winks hollering at one of the Mason ranch cowboys to "Circle around the thicket and look for any signs of her."

I slowed at the edge of the canyon, and glanced over to see Conrad spurring Ringo down the incline. "I see 'em, Mr. Winks. They're grazing in the canyon bottom!"

"Stay back, Conrad," yelled Mr. Winks.

But it was too late.

Conrad already had his lasso out building a loop, and Mr. Winks and the other men were too far behind to stop him.

It was up to me, and me alone, to protect Conrad!

I looked around and noticed a short cut to the canyon bottom, but it was rough, steep, and rocky. I had no choice. I ran as fast as I could without tumbling head first. I lunged forward and scooted down on my hindquarters thrusting my shoulders and burning my back hocks.

Mr. Mason and his cowboys were on one side of the canyon closing in. Mr. Winks, Doc Riley, and Mr. Barton came in from the other side. There was no way the men could get to her before Conrad.

He spurred Ringo as hard as he could, swinging his lasso, and yelling, "I'm gonna get you now, you mean old cow."

But, this was not Cowboy School, and this cow was no brow-beaten steer.

The cow and her calf ran away from Conrad and Ringo.

Whew, okay. She was going in the opposite direction of my little buddy.

But, then she stopped and spun around. Lowered her head and narrowed her eyes and looked at Ringo and Conrad as if she recognized Ringo.

She shook her horns, pawed the dirt, and charged straight at them. Her calf following right behind.

My heart leaped into my throat. I was still too far away to help. I kicked myself into a gallop, every part of my body in pain.

Ringo darted to the side just as she reached him and kicked at the calf the way he kicked at the steers at Cowboy School.

Except he dodged so fast that Conrad lost his balance. He was hanging on the side, clinging to the saddle horn. If he fell off…

No, I couldn't think that way. *Hang on, Conrad, I'm coming.*

The mama cow bellowed and ran between her calf and Ringo. She shook her horns at him. Ringo kicked at her. Conrad's grip of the saddle horn loosened. He tumbled off Ringo's back and fell into the dirt and rocks.

Ringo screamed and side kicked at the cow again, but she blocked his hoof with her big horns.

Conrad sat dazed on the ground, his hair matted with dirt, and his shirt ripped.

The cow spun and nostrils flaring, faced off with Ringo again.

Skittishly, he searched for a way out.

The calf flanked his left, a rock canyon wall on his right, Mama Cow straight ahead. Ringo's only out was behind him where Conrad struggled to get on his feet.

Mama Cow bellowed and lowered her head.

Ringo swiveled, ran toward Conrad, and on his way past, swung his hip into him, knocking Conrad to the ground, closer to the baby calf.

The tiger-striped cow stopped.

I remembered what Seven had told me about the mama cow being abused when she was a calf. Someone had been mean to her, so she'd turned mean herself.

She cast one last glance at the departing Ringo, then turned all her attention on Conrad. He was near enough to her baby to touch the little guy.

My heart flipped into my throat. Could I reach Conrad in time?

Mama Cow shook her horns and charged!

Conrad took off running to the nearest tree, but it was too far away. He stumbled, fell to the ground right in front of the cow.

I was almost there now. My shoulders were burning like fire, but I didn't care. I had to save Conrad, no matter what.

She was almost on top of Conrad. He flailed, trying to get back on his feet. I saw her horns flash.

"No!" I yelled.

The cow turned and stopped to check her bawling calf.

Conrad lay trembling on the ground. His eyes were exploding with fright. Her horns hadn't gotten him. She shook off the dust, lowered her head and came at him.

She raced toward Conrad, but I jumped in front of him and stood strong. I bared my teeth, backed both ears, and wheeled around for a strike. Letting her know I'd kick the stuffing out of her if I had to. But I wanted to try another way. A gentler way.

This time, she saw my determination.

She slowed, and came to a stop, not wanting more of my double-barreled kicks.

She stood staring at us, panting. Her eyes drooped and her shoulders dropped. She looked tired of fighting and running.

Slowly, I eased over to her calf. He was standing off to one side, crying for her.

I lowered my head and as gently as I could, nudged the calf toward its mama.

She trembled, fear in her eyes. She was scared I was going to hurt him.

I licked the calf's ear to show her it was safe for her calf to be around horses.

With a soft snort, the big horned tiger-striped cow eased up to her calf and let out an easy moo. She looked from me to Conrad and back to her baby.

I felt a strange tugging in my heart. All along, she'd only wanted to protect her calf the way I wanted to protect Conrad.

Our eyes locked, and we shared a look of mutual respect and understanding.

The men and their horses showed up. They surrounded the cow and her calf and tossed a soft loop around the cow's horns.

The mama cow didn't even try to fight her way out, she just stood there accepting her fate.

Conrad dusted himself off and looked at the men. "Please go easy on her. She's not scared anymore."

Mr. Mason rode up leading Ringo by the reins, "Conrad, I'm sorry to tell you, but your gonna have to find yourself

another horse, Ringo is going back to the remuda."
Conrad said, "Yes, sir." He walked over to Ringo, took his saddle and blankets."

I nudged his ear with my lip.

He took his lasso and put it around Ringo's neck and handed the other end to Mr. Mason. "I'll need my bridle, sir."

Conrad got me all saddled and bridled and put his foot in the stirrup.

Mr. Winks said, "I think we'll keep Mama Cow and her calf here at the Mesquite Bean for a week or two. I'll hand feed her and get her as gentle as a baby kitten before I turn her back with the other cows and their calves, then I'll try to find her owner."

Conrad rode up to Mr. Barton and held his hand out with thirty dollars in it. "This money doesn't belong to me and when we get back to the barn, I'll give you the halter. After seeing the way Ringo tried to bite that baby calf, I know he cheated the same way in the competition by biting those steers."

"Son, are you sure you want to do this?" Mr. Barton looked solemn.

"Yes, sir, I am. The real champion sorter is Ashley and Scarbutt. They didn't cheat."

Mr. Barton shook Conrad's hand. "I'll see you and Gunpowder at Cowboy School, Monday morning."

Conrad grinned and said, "You sure will! The Gunpowder and Conrad team is back!"

Mr. Winks drove the cow and her calf to the ranch, leaving the cowhands to ride back together.

Conrad had me go slowly, taking it easy on my shoulder, but I felt so good to have him back that I didn't notice the pain. I wanted to trot ahead with the others.

One of Mr. Mason's ranch cowboys looked over his shoulder at us, spun his horse around and loped back. He rode beside us, stuck his big, rough, hand out. "Howdy, Conrad, I'm Butch."

"Nice to meet you," Conrad said.

Butch slouched a little in the saddle like an old cowhand. "I've been a ranch cowboy for Mr. Mason and his family for a long time."

The old cowboy had a weathered face, rough hands, worn jeans, a tattered long sleeve shirt, and sweat stained cowboy hat. The kind of cowboy that was true, honest, hardworking, and listened more than he talked. He had a kind smile that made him likeable without even knowing him.

"Thanks for coming back to check on us," Conrad said.

They lapsed into a comfortable silence.

Butch looked over at Conrad, tilted his hat back on his head, and ran his big hand over his eyes. "I saw everything back at the Canyon. I was sitting high on the bluff looking down."

"Yes, sir?" replied Conrad.

"You've got one heck of a cowpony there, Conrad."

"Yes, sir, I know that I've got some making up to do. Gunpowder saved my life!"

Butch stopped his horse and looked at Conrad. His smile had evened out and his gray eyes locked on to Conrad's. "Son, I've been sitting in the saddle nearly my whole life. I've ridden a lot of horses, some belonged to me and some belonged to the ranch. The good ones will teach you a thing or two, and I want to share something that I haven't told many people."

"What's that, sir?"

"A cowhand can never own a cowpony like Gunpowder. They will just pick you out and let you join up with them because they love you. They will give you a hard day's work on the ranch and give all they have in the arena. They will risk their life for you."

Conrad leaned over and scratched behind my ears. I was so happy, I thought my heart might burst.

"You have one of those rare horses. You have a friend."

"Yes sir, you are right. Gunpowder never quit me, but I

quit him. I got wrapped up in trying to win and forgot about what is most important. Being a friend to my best friend, Gunpowder."

Butch smiled. "Now you're talking like a real cowboy."

Acknowledgement

I would like to acknowledge and thank my wife Jennifer, son Riley, and mother Caroline for their constant encouragement and support. I would also like to thank my amazing writing coach New York Times and USA Today Best Selling Author Lori Wilde. A special thank you to Aubrey Keim for sharing her knowledge from working in a vet clinic.

Be sure to check out *Gunpowder's* website at
www.gunpowderandconrad.com
for the latest newsletter, upcoming information on the next
Gunpowder book, and how to order other
books in the *Gunpowder* series.

RIVALS ON THE RANCH
GUNPOWDER

Author Michael Rountree

Michael Rountree and his wife Jennifer live and teach school in Spearman, Texas. Gunpowder, Rivals on the Ranch is the third book in the Gunpowder series which grew from a desire to interest his students in learning by finding common ground- horses.

Illustrator Peyton Aufill

Peyton Aufill is a painter, photographer and graphic designer in Canadian, Texas. He is married to a wonderful, supportive wife, Kimberly, who cheers him on in all of his endeavors. To find out more about his work, you can visit Aufill's website at conejogallery.com.